ARY

Ever After High™

Once Upon a Pet

A Collection of Little Pet Stories

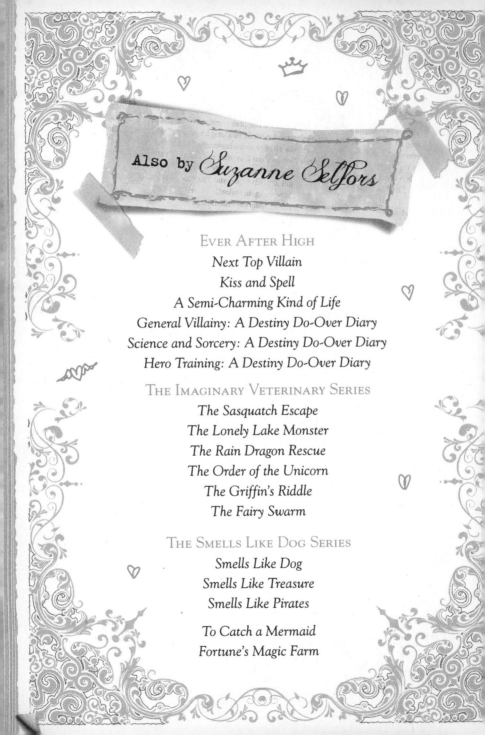

Also by *Suzanne Selfors*

Ever After High™

EVER AFTER Royals!

Once Upon a Pet

A Collection of Little Pet Stories

EVER AFTER Rebels

Suzanne Selfors

LB

LITTLE, BROWN AND COMPANY

NEW YORK   BOSTON

Copyright © 2015 Mattel, Inc.

"Duchess Swan and the Next Top Bird: A Little Pirouette Story" © 2014 Mattel, Inc.

Little, Brown and Company

Hachette Book Group
1290 Avenue of the Americas, New York, NY 10104
Visit us at lb-kids.com

Little, Brown and Company is a division of Hachette Book Group, Inc. The Little, Brown name and logo are trademarks of Hachette Book Group, Inc.

The publisher is not responsible for websites (or their content) that are not owned by the publisher.

First Edition: October 2015
"Duchess Swan and the Next Top Bird: A Little Pirouette Story,"
"Lizzie Hearts and the Hedgehog's Hexcellent Adventure: A Little Shuffle Story,"
"Ginger Breadhouse and the Candy Fish Wish: A Little Jelly Story,"
"Hopper Croakington II and the Princely Present: A Little Drake Story,"
"Dexter Charming and the Trouble with Jackalopes: A Little Mr. Cottonhorn Story,"
and "Darling Charming and the Horse of a Different Color: A Little Sir Gallopad Story" originally published as digital original editions
by Little, Brown and Company.

Library of Congress Control Number: 2015945871

ISBN 978-0-316-26481-5

10 9 8 7 6 5 4 3 2 1

RRD-C

Printed in the United States of America

Contents

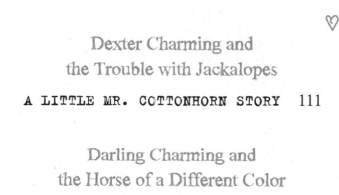

Duchess Swan
and the
Next Top Bird

A Little

Pirouette Story

*O*nce upon a sunny day, a swan sat in her nest, peacefully napping. This was no ordinary nest hidden among dreary weeds, nor set beside a commonplace pond. This nest was located in the girls' dormitory at Ever After High, a boarding school for the sons and daughters of fairytale characters. On the first day of school, the nest had been delivered to the bedroom of Duchess Swan, daughter of the Swan Princess. It had been specially woven for her beautiful pet trumpeter, Pirouette.

Napping was one of Pirouette's favorite activities, but on this particular day, the sound of stomping footsteps disturbed her slumber. She lazily opened her black eyes. *What is that racket?* The footsteps grew louder, then two girls stormed into the bedroom.

"Can you believe what he said?" Duchess asked, her voice cracking with emotion. She was talking to her roommate, Lizzie Hearts, daughter of the Queen of Hearts.

"It's to be hexpected," Lizzie told her. "Daring Charming's favorite topic of conversation is *Daring Charming*. Did you read his latest MirrorBlog entry? He rated himself on charm, charisma, and cuteness. All tens, of course." She tossed her book bag onto her messy bed. "Turn the page and forget about him."

Pirouette straightened her long neck. Normally, she wouldn't be interested in the chitter-chatter across the room. The girls had too many toils and troubles, secrets and squabbles to keep track of. Royal princesses were so complicated. It seemed as if there was one drama after another. Being a swan was much simpler. Usually, the biggest problem Pirouette faced was whether she should preen her left wing first or her right wing. But something was different today. Duchess seemed very upset. Her fists were clenched and she was pacing the length of the room. This worried Pirouette because when Duchess was unhappy, things tended to happen. Duchess wasn't the kind of princess who let people walk over her. Neither was Lizzie. So Pirouette blinked away the haze of sleep and listened intently to the goings-on.

"Daring actually said that *his* bird is more talented than *my* bird!" Duchess's lavender, black, and white hair swooshed with each frustrated step. "How can he think such a thing? The only thing *his* peacock does is strut around, but *my* swan can dance. How can he compare the two?"

Pirouette nodded in full agreement. Anyone could strut. It took no talent whatsoever. But Pirouette was the only bird at Ever After High who knew enough ballet moves to dance a *pas de deux*. She'd learned over the years by watching Duchess's ballet practices. Her favorite move was the arabesque, which required her to balance on one leg with her wings outstretched.

"Daring Charming really flusters my feathers!" Duchess exclaimed. "He's so...so..."

"So full of himself," Lizzie said with a determined *hmph*.

"Yes. Full of himself." Duchess sank onto the edge of her bed. Then she sighed, and her expression changed from angry to dreamy. "But he's so...cute. Why does he have to be so cute?" Pirouette had noticed that whenever Duchess talked about the boy named Daring, she was either upset with him or gushing over him. She'd been crushing on him ever since school began, but he'd never shown any interest in her. "It's bad enough he never notices *me*, but now he's insulting my beautiful swan." Her shoulders drooped, along with the white feathers in her headpiece.

Recognizing the twinge of hurt in Duchess's voice, Pirouette stepped out of her nest. Then she pressed

the top of her head against Duchess's hand. *Don't feel sad*, she said, but it came out as "*Honk!*"

Duchess ran her hand down the swan's neck. "You're the most talented bird at this school. You make Daring's peacock look like a dodo."

Pirouette wasn't sure what a dodo was, but it didn't sound very smart. So she nodded in agreement.

Then a mischievous grin spread across Duchess's face. "I know what I'll do. I'll show him."

"Yes! Show him!" Lizzie said with a wave of her scepter. "Now you're talking like a Royal. Off with his head! His big blond head!"

Heads wouldn't roll—that wasn't Duchess's style. But something would be done to prove her point. Pirouette wagged her little tail and looked into Duchess's eyes. That glimmer was very familiar. Her girl was planning something.

Duchess began pacing again. "Daring is the most handsome and the most popular prince on campus, right?"

"Well, he sure thinks he is."

"And he wins every competition he enters, right?"

Lizzie snorted. "*That* is definitely true."

Duchess spun on her heels and pointed a finger in the air. "Well, he's not going to win *this* time. I have the top bird on campus, and I'm going to prove it." She wrapped an arm around Pirouette. "I mean, *we're* going to prove it."

"*Honk?*"

Late that afternoon, Pirouette glided across her favorite Ever After High pond, sunlight warming her back. Purple flowers sat atop lily pads like cupcakes on platters. Sparkling water sprayed from the unicorn fountain. As students walked past, their conversations did not draw the swan's attention. She was much more interested in the little bugs that darted between the reeds. Those wiggly tidbits were tasty treats.

"Pirouette!" a familiar voice called.

She swallowed a bug, then glanced across the pond. Duchess waved at her from the other end. Pirouette smiled. Sometimes Duchess brought little treats from the Castleteria. With a kick of her legs, Pirouette pushed through the lilies. When she reached the water's edge, she stepped onto land and waddled up to Duchess's shiny laced shoes. "Honk!" She wagged her tail, watching the ground for falling crumbs.

"We'd better hurry," Duchess told her. "It'll be starting soon." She began to walk away, hexting on her MirrorPhone at the same time.

No crumbs? After a little hiss of disappointment, Pirouette shook her feathers dry, then followed as quickly as she could, her webbed feet leaving damp prints on the stone path. It was too late in the day for ballet lessons, so where was Duchess leading her? "Honk?"

"Don't worry. It's a surprise," Duchess said mischievously. "But you'll see soon enough." Her Mirror-Phone chimed. "Oh, hexcellent! Lizzie's bringing the music. Everything's in order. I'm getting mother-goosebumps just thinking about our victory!"

Pirouette had no idea what was going on. Music? Victory? Where were the snacks?

A few minutes later, she followed Duchess into the Charmitorium. Pirouette had never been inside this large performance hall. Students were streaming in, quickly filling the seats that faced the gilded stage. A banner hung from the carved rafters:

FEATHERED FRIENDS TALENT SHOW

"Isn't this great?" Duchess said with a dramatic flourish of her arm. "All these people came to see you dance."

Pirouette stopped in her tracks. Her heartbeat doubled. Dance on that stage? With everyone watching? Her legs felt frozen. She'd never performed for anyone. She'd only danced in the studio with Duchess. Just the two of them. Just for fun. But at that moment, Duchess was climbing onto the stage and motioning for Pirouette to join her. Voices echoed off the walls as students continued to take their seats. They'd all be looking at her? She got so nervous a few feathers fell out—and it wasn't even molting season!

Pirouette wanted to fly out the door and make her escape back to the pond.

"Did somebody misplace a duck?" a voice asked.

Pirouette looked around. What was he talking about? There was no duck to be seen. Suddenly, two hands grabbed her and lifted her into the air. Then the hands set her down, closer to the wall. "Nice duck," the voice said as a hand patted her head.

There were three things that made Pirouette throw a hissy fit—polluted water, bird hunters, and being called a *duck*. She knew many ducks. They were simple creatures who liked to stick their heads underwater and their bottoms in the air. Some were nice, some were bothersome. But one thing could be said about all ducks—they were *not* swans. And Pirouette was the grandest of all swans—a trumpeter.

She glared at the boy who had picked her up and called her a duck. It was Daring Charming, the prince who made Duchess flip her crown every time she saw him. After nearly blinding Pirouette with his smile, he ran a hand over his tussled blond locks. "Hello, ladies," he called, waving at a group of girls. They giggled and waved back. Each girl wore a T-shirt with Daring's face plastered on the front. "I see my fan club has arrived." His large, polished boots barely missed Pirouette's delicate feet as he strode up the aisle. That was when she noticed the bird who was following the prince.

His name was P-Hawk, a large male peacock who lived at the school. Pirouette had only seen him from a distance. Because he wasn't waterfowl, P-Hawk didn't hang out in the ponds. He liked to roost in the highest branches of the campus trees. The blues and greens in his feathers were even more vibrant up close. He winked at Pirouette as he strutted by.

Still fuming about the "duck" comment, Pirouette hissed at him.

"Pirouette!" Duchess called from the stage. But Pirouette didn't budge. There was no way she was going to dance in front of *everyone*. She shuddered nervously, and another feather fell out.

"Everyone, move out of my way!" Lizzie ordered as she pushed between students. As the daughter of the Queen of Hearts, she was used to issuing commands. Then she looked down at Pirouette. "Why aren't you on the stage?"

Duchess hurried back down the aisle. "She won't budge. We'll have to carry her."

Pirouette tried to escape, but she wasn't fast enough. She honked as the girls reached around her midsection and lifted her. "She's trembling," Lizzie said. "I think she's scared." They set her down at the edge of the stage.

Duchess knelt next to Pirouette and gently held her feathered face with both hands. "Don't worry," she told her. "All dancers get stage fright. But once you step into the spotlight, you'll feel better. Believe me. All you have to do is dance, and everyone will see that you're the most talented bird at Ever After High. They'll love you. And Daring Charming will have to eat his words."

"My mother made me eat words in Wonderland," Lizzie said. "They're supposed to be nutritious."

Pirouette didn't know what words tasted like. But what she did know was that the Charmitorium was so crowded that students were now standing in the aisles. Her stomach felt bad, like the time she'd eaten too many slugs.

Duchess ran a hand down Pirouette's back. "You're still trembling." She glanced over at Daring and his strutting peacock. They were both admiring themselves in a mirror. Duchess groaned. "Even though Daring needs to be taught a lesson, I won't make you do this, Pirouette. I don't want you to feel scared. If you want, we can leave."

Pirouette thought about it. She had nothing to prove. She was happy in her pond. Happy in her nest. Who cared what this boy thought? And what if that pompous peacock laughed at her? Birds aren't supposed to dance. She wanted to tuck her head under her wing.

But then she saw the expression on P-Hawk's face.

He was smirking at her. And with his foot, he drew the word *duck* on the stage floor.

Oh, it's on, she thought.

"Honk!"

---

elcome, students, to the very first Feathered Friends Talent Show," a rather bushy man bellowed from center stage. He didn't need a microphone. His voice sounded as if it had been recorded inside a cave. Pirouette had seen him before. His name was Professor Poppa Bear. "I guess I'm the judge of this contest because I'm the only Beast Training and Care teacher at Ever After High. And also because the Charming family said that if I do it, they'll give me a year's supply of my favorite snack." He pointed to a stack of boxes, each marked INSTANT PORRIDGE.

"Hey, that's bribery," Duchess complained.

Professor Poppa Bear ignored her. "Let's get this contest started. I wanna get back to my not-too-big-and-not-too-small recliner and watch the bookball game."

Pirouette shuffled nervously. Four students and their birds had gathered onstage. Each student sat on a stool. Daring Charming was the first student. He wore a confident smile, as did P-Hawk, who'd settled at the prince's boots. Another boy, whose head was very round and whose skin was as smooth and white as an eggshell, sat on the second stool. He wobbled as if he was having trouble keeping his balance. The chicken that was tucked under his arm kept squawking. A princess who also lived in the girls' dormitory sat on the third stool. Her bird was sleeping in a golden basket. Duchess sat on the fourth stool, Pirouette at her feet.

"Who's first?" Professor Poppa Bear hollered.

"Ladies first," Daring said. He smiled at the audience, and a whole row of girls fainted. Another row was momentarily blinded by his brilliant teeth.

The other princess carried her golden basket and bird to center stage. "Hello," she said to the audience. "As most of you know, my name is Ashlynn Ella." Her long strawberry-blond hair was held back with a ribbon. "When Duchess told me that she wanted to have a bird talent show, I was hexstatic. I think we should pay more attention to our feathered friends and live in harmony with nature." She set the basket on the floor. "I'd like to introduce you to my bird, Sandella."

A red-and-orange bird stepped out of the basket. Her tail was twice as long as her body. "Sandella is a phoenix," Ashlynn explained. "Her talent is that she can burst into flames and then be reborn." Ashlynn stepped back, giving the bird lots of room. "Behold."

This was very interesting. Pirouette straightened her neck. There was no way she could compete with bursting into flames and being reborn. She might not have to dance after all, which would make her very happy. But it wouldn't prove to P-Hawk that she had amazing talent and was in no way related to a duck.

As Sandella stood perfectly still, looking out at the audience, Professor Poppa Bear ran offstage, returning a moment later with a fire extinguisher. Silence descended as everyone watched and waited. Sandella blinked. The audience held their breath. Sandella clicked her beak. Everyone gasped. Then, with an uppity flick of her tail, the phoenix returned to her golden basket and closed her eyes. Nothing had happened.

Ashlynn shrugged. "I guess she's not in the mood to burst into flames. I'm royally sorry." With the basket in hand, she returned to her stool. The audience grumbled with disappointment.

"Next!" Professor Poppa Bear hollered.

"It's our turn," Duchess whispered. She gave Pirouette a little push of encouragement. But the swan wouldn't move. "Pirouette? It's time to dance. Don't you want to do this? Everyone's watching."

Yes, everyone's watching. Pirouette wanted to prove her talent, but her legs didn't seem to be working. She'd never felt so scared. *Please let me go back to the pond.* This was the worst moment of her life!

"I think she has stage fright," Ashlynn said with concern.

"No, she doesn't," Duchess insisted. "She just needs a little more time to get ready. We'll go last."

Would time cure her stage fright? Pirouette sure hoped so, because if any more of her feathers fell out, she might be mistaken for a seagull.

"I'll go next," said the roundheaded boy. He scooted off his stool and stumbled to center stage. He set his chicken on the floor, then waved at the audience. "Hello. My name is Humphrey Dumpty, and this is my chicken, Benedict. He's a king."

The chicken, who wore a golden crown, rustled his feathers, then began walking in a circle.

Professor Poppa Bear scratched his shaggy neck. "You mean he's a rooster?"

"No, he's a king chicken," Humphrey said.

"What's his talent?" Professor Poppa Bear asked.

"You'll see." Humphrey stuck two fingers in his mouth and whistled. The chicken squawked loudly, squatted, and laid a white egg. "Ta-da," Humphrey said with a proud smile. "He laid an egg."

"He?" Professor Poppa Bear shook his head. "Son, I think you might be a bit confused."

As the audience roared with laughter, Humphrey returned to his stool. Duchess pressed her mouth close to Pirouette's ear. "The phoenix did nothing and the chicken laid an egg. You're sure to win this."

"Next!"

Daring Charming stood. He unbuttoned his letterman's jacket, then strode to center stage. "Hello, fellow fairytales," he said in a deep, clear voice. "There is no need for me to introduce myself, since my autographed headshot is the bestseller at the Ever After High Bookstore." He chuckled proudly. "By the way, my personalized calendar will be arriving soon. You lucky ladies can have me hanging on

your wall January through December." The girls who had previously fainted and then recovered fainted again.

Pirouette didn't care about Daring collectibles. All she could think about was that big stage, with the spotlight shining, and all those faces watching. She glanced at the basket. What would the phoenix think when Pirouette began dancing? What would the king chicken think? And, most especially, what would that super-gorgeous peacock think? She pressed against Duchess's leg. When would this be over?

"Get on with it, Mr. Charming," Professor Poppa Bear said grumpily.

Daring clapped his hands and P-Hawk stepped to center stage. He stood facing the audience. He looked left. He looked right. Then—*whoosh*—he opened his tail.

Pirouette honked with surprise. She'd seen peacock tails before, but never one so large! It unfolded like a giant's fan. Long, elegant feathers pointed toward the ceiling, each painted with a sparkling black eye. The audience clapped with appreciation as P-Hawk strutted about, showing off his plumage.

"Oh feather dusters," Duchess grumbled.

"Very impressive," Professor Poppa Bear said.

"Enchanting," Ashlynn added.

Humphrey Dumpty didn't say anything. He was too busy trying not to fall off the stool.

"There's no need to continue the contest," Daring declared. "P-Hawk is undoubtedly the most talented bird at Ever After High."

"Agreed," Professor Poppa Bear said. "I guess we're done here. I've got just enough time to get home and watch the fourth chapter of the game." He started to leave.

"Wait," Duchess called. She hurried to center stage and stood in the spotlight. "What about my swan? She still needs to compete."

Professor Poppa Bear growled with disappointment. "Very well. But be quick about it."

Daring shrugged. Then he returned to his stool. As P-Hawk strutted past Pirouette, he smirked again. Pirouette's heart beat doubly fast.

"Music," Duchess called.

"That's me!" Lizzie announced from the front row. She opened her MirrorPad, and the sound track from Tchaikovsky's *Swan Lake* blasted from the speaker. It was an important ballet for Duchess because it was the story of a princess who was cursed by a sorcerer and turned into a swan. That story was Duchess's destiny. She and Pirouette had danced to it many times over the years. Pirouette knew the moves by heart.

Duchess motioned at her, a proud smile on her face. "Come on, Pirouette. Show everyone that *you* are the most talented bird." By everyone, she meant *Daring*, of course. P-Hawk rolled his eyes and faked a yawn.

Oh, I'll show him! Slowly, step-by-step, as if her webbed feet were made of lead, Pirouette inched toward the spotlight. With her eyes narrowed against the brightness, she could no longer see the faces of those watching. The music flowed from Lizzie's speakers, filling every inch of the Charmitorium.

"Go ahead," Duchess encouraged. "Arabesque."

Here I go. After a deep breath, Pirouette stretched her wings, then rose onto one leg, balancing perfectly as she always did. Then she stepped forward, one, two, three, and rose onto the other leg, her wings outstretched like a ballerina's arms. The audience *ooh*ed and *aah*ed. It was going well. She glanced over at P-Hawk. He was watching, wide-eyed, but not laughing. Duchess was beaming. Another step, one, two, three, and—

Pirouette tumbled forward, waddling like a duck and landing at the edge of the stage.

Everyone gasped.

She lowered her head in humiliation. That arrogant peacock would win just because he'd been born with a nice tail. She'd failed. She was about to tuck her head under her wing when the audience began to clap. Pirouette sat up and turned around.

King Benedict had shuffled to center stage and was dancing. He didn't know any ballet moves, but he certainly knew how to keep rhythm to the music. He bobbed his head and made a happy *cluck, cluck* sound. Then the golden basket wobbled, and the phoenix raced forward. She joined in the dance, swishing her tail feathers along the floor and kicking out her feet. And then P-Hawk was at Pirouette's side. He didn't smirk, and he didn't roll his eyes. He winked, then nudged her with his beak, urging her to get up. She did, and the two of them walked into the spotlight, joining the others. P-Hawk bowed, then opened his tail with a mighty *swoosh*. He strutted around Pirouette, smiling at her. She couldn't believe it. All the birds were dancing, and the audience loved it. Applause filled the air. Her confidence renewed, Pirouette stretched her wings and rose onto one leg. The audience cheered.

Daring, Duchess, Humphrey, and Ashlynn gathered around Professor Poppa Bear.

"Who's the winner?" Duchess asked.

"Need you ask?" Daring said. "Clearly, my bird is the best dancer."

"Hexcuse me?" Duchess put her hands on her hips. "That's so not true. My swan knows how to do a *grand jeté*."

"I think they're all good dancers," Ashlynn said.

"Everyone wins!" Professor Poppa Bear hollered. "Now, get out of my way so I can go watch the game. Don't anyone tell me the score!" And he rushed down the aisle and out the exit.

"Everyone wins?" Duchess and Daring said at the same time. Pirouette stopped dancing and watched her girl. Duchess and Daring stood face-to-face, arguing about whose bird was more talented.

"I order everyone to stop arguing!" Lizzie commanded. Then, with a playful smile, she touched her MirrorPad. *Swan Lake* stopped playing, and a pop tune by Katy Fairy filled the Charmitorium. King Benedict, Sandella, and P-Hawk kicked up their feet, prancing, jumping, and twirling to the happy beat. Lizzie jumped up onstage and started

dancing with them. The entire front row joined her, and soon the stage was full of dancers.

Even though she was surrounded by lots of people, Pirouette couldn't resist the rhythm. The music's drum track vibrated up her legs. She moved from side to side, her little tail wagging.

Duchess smiled down at her and patted her head. "I'm so proud of you. You got over your stage fright!" Pirouette stretched her wings and twirled.

"Perhaps my bird isn't the most talented after all," Daring said with astonishment as Pirouette pointed her toes and leaped.

Lizzie whispered in Duchess's ear. "I think Daring just *ate his words*." They both giggled.

Then Duchess started dancing. And so did Daring.

As P-Hawk circled around Pirouette, his head feathers bobbing, no one seemed to care who the best bird was. And best of all, everyone was having fun.

When King Benedict laid another egg, everyone laughed.

"*Honk!*"

Lizzie Hearts and the Hedgehog's Hexcellent Adventure

A Little Shuffle Story

*A*t a very special school called Ever After High, in the dormitory room of the Queen of Hearts's daughter, a little hedgehog named Shuffle was fast asleep.

In many ways, Shuffle was like other hedgehogs. She liked to snooze most of the day, usually curled up in a warm spot, hidden from view. She liked to forage most of the night, looking for yummy stuff to eat—anything with six or eight legs that crawled across the floor was acceptable, but sweet treats were preferred. When happy, she made soft grunting sounds, and when scared, she rolled into a tight

ball and turned herself into a prickly pincushion—a literal royal pain!

But Shuffle wasn't exactly ordinary, because she'd been born in Wonderland, an amazing, faraway kingdom where very little made sense and very much made no sense. As she napped, she dreamed about her homeland. She imagined the heart-shaped hedgerows outside the queen's palace, where her family lived. Her mother and father were employed as croquet balls, which is not as painful as it sounds, mostly because the queen had terrible aim and was always missing.

As these memories filled her head, Shuffle snorted happily in her sleep, because Wonderland was where she'd developed her sweet tooth. Whenever the queen rode past, her card soldiers would toss treats such as frosted tea cakes, sugar hearts, and Cheshire chocolates to the flocks of flamingos. The hedge-hogs would waddle between flamingo legs, snuffling the crumbs. Getting poked by a long flamingo beak was worth the risk because those treats were wonderlicious.

One day, while Shuffle foraged for tea cake crumbs with her family, her life changed forever. "Listen up! Listen up!" the Queen of Hearts bellowed. "My daughter, Her Royal Highness Princess Lizzie, wants a pet hedgehog! And what my daughter wants, my daughter gets! So line up, you portly little pricklebugs, or heads will roll!"

"Make sure your snouts are clean," Mother Hedgehog told her twenty-seven children. "It's an honor to be chosen by a princess. You'll get to live in the palace." While the queen glared at them, her face as red as the painted roses, the hedgehog siblings lined up.

"Go on!" the queen hollered in her shrill voice. "Choose one!"

Lizzie Hearts marched past the trembling hedgehogs, her red boots leaving imprints in the soft grass. "I want that one!" Lizzie said with a wave of her scepter. "No, wait, I want that one! No, I've changed my mind. That one!" Snuffle didn't really care about the goings-on, because she'd spied a large crumb near one of the rosebushes. Her mouth began to water.

Forget this, Shuffle thought. *That crumb has my name on it.* And off she waddled.

"That one!" Lizzie cried. Before Shuffle could roll into a prickly ball, she was hoisted into the air. And before she could wiggle free, she found herself being put headfirst into a Puss-in-Boots Couture handbag. "She won't fit!" Lizzie exclaimed. "Her belly's too big."

"Off with her head!" the Queen of Hearts ordered.

"Now, Mother, I don't think that's necessary. She simply needs to stop eating so much sugar." Lizzie tucked Shuffle in the crook of her arm and patted her little spiky head. That was when Shuffle noticed the tower of luggage heaped on top of a nearby carriage. As it turned out, the palace wasn't Shuffle's destination. Lizzie was leaving for Ever After High, and Shuffle was going with her, like it or not. Good-bye, family. Good-bye, hedgerow.

Good-bye, tea cakes, sugar hearts, and Cheshire chocolates!

Shuffle's dream about that fateful day faded away and was replaced by the image of a big bowl of Farmer-in-the-Dell brand granola. Granola was so boring! But ever since coming to Ever After High, Lizzie had insisted that Shuffle eat healthy snacks.

As night fell over the school, Shuffle waited at the bottom of the bed for Lizzie to fall asleep. It was warm down beneath the quilts. She liked curling up next to the fuzzy socks that Lizzie often slept in. The sound of Lizzie's snoring was her cue to emerge. Wiggling her round bottom, she waddled up the mattress until she reached Lizzie's head. Poking her nose out of the blankets, she glanced over at the window to make sure darkness had settled. A little shiver of anticipation tickled the tips of her spines. It was time to forage! Forget the granola. She wanted the sweet taste of Wonderland.

Careful not to step on Lizzie's face or poke her with a quill, Shuffle climbed around Lizzie's head and then free-fell off the side of the bed, landing softly in a pile of socks. Lizzie's side of the dormitory room was always messy, which was great for a hedgehog because there were plenty of places to burrow and hide in. And occasionally get stepped on, which wasn't so nice. But that's what happens when you're smaller than everyone else.

The other girl who shared the room was named Duchess Swan, daughter of the Swan Princess, and she was also fast asleep, her lavender quilt rising and falling with her deep breaths. The white swan who slept in a nest next to Duchess's bed raised her head and blinked at Shuffle. Her name was Pirouette. She wasn't nocturnal, so she never joined Shuffle on these evening strolls. She wasn't invited anyway. Shuffle didn't like the swan, who had a snooty air about her, as if she were better just because she was taller and could fly. And the swan was very protective of her nest, sitting on it as if it were a throne. If Shuffle got too close, Pirouette would throw a hissy fit. So whenever Pirouette left the dorm room to go for a swim or stretch her wings, Shuffle used the nest as a wastebasket, tossing in peanut shells and corn kernels that had gone stale. And bits of that terrible Farmer-in-the-Dell granola!

On this night, Shuffle ignored Pirouette's stare and continued on her journey. *Don't worry. I won't get near your precious nest,* Shuffle thought, sticking her snout in the air as she passed by. The swan hissed quietly, then tucked her shiny black beak under her wing and closed her eyes.

Around piles of clothing and across the room Shuffle waddled until she reached the dorm room door. When she and Lizzie had moved in, a nice boy named Hunter Huntsman had installed a hedgehog door so Shuffle could come and go as she pleased. All she had to do was push against the flap and slip through.

The hallway was quiet. Shuffle sat on her haunches for a moment, looking around. One of the other princesses had a snow fox who sometimes prowled at night. As the fox had learned, a hedgehog might *look* fat and delectable, but getting past all those spines was no fun at all.

Keeping close to the wall, Shuffle scurried down the hallway, her snout sniffing. Two succulent spiders were ignored, as was a juicy housefly. *Forget them.* Something better was waiting, and she could smell it. Her little legs picked up their pace as the aroma got closer. Then she threw out her legs and skidded on her belly, stopping right in front of the door of the dorm room that belonged to Ginger Breadhouse. Ginger was the daughter of the Candy Witch, but she was very nice and was known throughout the school as a hexcellent cook—masterful in her baking abilities.

A tiny box sat on the floor. A gift tag was attached. It read:

FOR SHUFFLE. DON'T EAT IT ALL AT ONCE.

Shuffle sat on her bottom and clapped her little paws with glee. A present for her! Ginger liked to make treats for the other students, and she'd bring them back to the dormitory to share. Last week, when Ginger brought hot cross buns, Shuffle had jettisoned herself off a chair and landed smack-dab in the middle of the tray, eating as fast as she could. "Isn't that cute?" Ginger had said. "She likes my baking." And so, before going to bed, Ginger began leaving a special hedgehog-sized snack outside her door. What would it be tonight? A cinnamon troll? A caramel castle? A chocolate kiss?

Using her snout, Shuffle pushed the present on its side. The lid tumbled off. She stuck her head inside the box and grunted happily. A waffle shaped like a throne awaited her, crispy on the outside and doughy everywhere else. Ignoring Ginger's instructions, Shuffle ate the whole thing. She wanted to curl up and take a nap right there, but if she did, Lizzie might come looking and find out that her hedgehog was being very naughty. So even though her tummy was so full it dragged on the floor, Shuffle waddled back to her own room. She left the box behind, hoping Ginger would fill it with another treat tomorrow night.

Pirouette raised her long neck and watched as Shuffle pushed back through the hedgehog door. Upon seeing the waffle crumbs that dotted Shuffle's snout, the swan shook her head disapprovingly. Shuffle grumbled at her, which meant *Mind your own business*. Too tired to climb back onto Lizzie's bed, Shuffle burrowed beneath a red scarf on the floor outside Lizzie's closet. She fell into a deep, satisfied sleep. Her tummy was happy. And so was she.

"*H*onk!"

Dawn had come, and Pirouette was waiting by the window to be let out. Why did birds have to announce that the sun was rising? Shuffle thought it was very rude. Sometimes she got so mad she'd throw pieces of her granola at Pirouette. But this morning she had no energy. She squirmed, trying to find a more comfortable position beneath the red scarf. She felt very strange.

"Wait," Duchess said to her swan. "I got this ribbon for you. It looks beautiful against your white feathers." Then Shuffle heard the window open and Pirouette's wings flapping as the swan flew off to find her favorite morning food—the soft spring grass that grew in the school's garden. Soon after she left, the dormitory filled with the sounds of morning. Lizzie complained as she searched through her closet, trying to find this or that. Duchess's quill scratched across the pages of her diary. Thumps and muffled voices came from beyond the walls, where the other girls were getting ready for the day.

But a new sound arose, louder than the others. *Rrrrrrumble.*

"What in Ever After was that?" Lizzie asked. The sound had been so loud it had bothered Shuffle's ears. And it was coming from nearby. *Rrrrrrumble.*

"It's under here," Duchess said as she picked up the red scarf.

Shuffle opened her eyes and found that both Lizzie and Duchess were leaning over, staring at her. Lizzie's black hair tumbled around her face in a carefree way, while Duchess's hair—long, with lavender, white, and black stripes—was perfectly combed and tied back with a strand of pearls.

The rumble sounded again. *What is that?* Shuffle wondered. *Make it go away.*

"It's coming from there," Lizzie said. She poked a fingertip against Shuffle's bloated belly. Shuffle squeaked and rolled into a ball.

"Shuffle? What's the matter with you?" Lizzie knelt and pressed her nose right up against the hedgehog's snout. "Wait a spell! You smell like sugar!" Lizzie picked a waffle crumb off Shuffle's face and inspected it. Then she scowled. "You're in hextreme trouble, young lady. You know you're not supposed to be sneaking treats."

Shuffle moaned. Her belly had never felt so grumpy. It rumbled three times in a row. Maybe she shouldn't have eaten the *entire* waffle throne.

"If she's sick, she should go see Professor Poppa Bear," Duchess said. The professor taught the Beast Training and Care class at Ever After High. He had the most experience with the assorted creatures, both magical and nonmagical, that lived at the school. "Maybe he can give her some medicine."

Medicine? Never ever! Shuffle curled up as tight as she could and stiffened all her quills.

"Ouch!" Lizzie cried as she tried to pick her up. "Uncurl yourself right now!"

No! Shuffle grunted. If they'd leave her alone, she could go back to sleep and dream about happy things, and then her tummy would surely feel better. She'd dream about the green croquet fields of Wonderland. The rows of red and white roses. Her family rooting around the hedge, snuffling up big, fat crumbs.

A flapping sound filled the room as Pirouette soared back through the window. She landed with a *thunk* on the bedroom floor.

"Oh, rabbit pellets!" Lizzie said as she tried, once again, to grab her prickly pet. "You're being very,

very naughty. How am I supposed to carry you to Professor Papa Bear?"

"How about wearing mittens?" Duchess suggested. "The three little kittens are always leaving theirs behind. I bet there's a pair in the Lost and Crowned Office."

"Hexcellent idea. But where's the Lost and Crowned Office?"

"I'll show you," Duchess said.

Lizzie pointed at Pirouette. "Keep an eye on her," she ordered the swan. "We'll be right back."

The door opened and closed, and the girls' footsteps faded down the hallway.

Rrrrrrumble.

"*Honk!*" A hard beak pushed against Shuffle's quills.

Shuffle lifted her head and opened her eyes. Pirouette stood over her, the lavender ribbon still tied around her neck. *What are you looking at? Go away,* Shuffle grumbled. She rolled over, but the swan simply walked around to the other side and poked her with her beak again. Shuffle ignored her. The rumbling grew louder. But then a sweet scent drifted up her snout. Pirouette had grabbed a left-over blade of spring grass from her breakfast bowl and had dropped it onto the carpet right next to Shuffle. The swan nudged the grass closer, then nodded.

Shuffle's tummy hurt too much to eat anything. She started to curl up again, but Pirouette stomped her webbed feet and honked and honked and honked. It felt like an alarm in Shuffle's head.

Okay, okay! I'll eat it! Just stop making all that noise. Pirouette settled down and watched as Shuffle nibbled the blade. It tasted bitter, but her stomach felt better. The rumbling, however, continued. Shuffle rose to her feet and looked around. There were no more grass blades. She pointed to the window. *Go get more.* She wiggled her bottom. Then she looked toward the doorway. The girls would be back with the mittens soon. And that meant…medicine!

Pirouette lowered herself onto her belly and

stretched out her left wing. Then she gently tapped her outstretched wing against the floor.

Shuffle didn't understand. Why was Pirouette nodding at her? Why was she pointing to her flattened back? Why wouldn't she go and get more grass? Shuffle winced as a sharp pain filled her tummy. *Rrrumble*.

Suddenly, with a swoop of her wing, Pirouette scooped the hedgehog off the carpet. And before Shuffle could squeak for help, the swan was in the air.

And flying out the window with Shuffle on board!

Shuffle grabbed the ends of the lavender ribbon, holding on for dear life. The dorm room disappeared, replaced by treetops and clouds. She squeezed her eyes shut. Hedgehog bellies are supposed to be pressed against the ground, not against a bird's back! But the feathers were surprisingly soft and warm. And the motion was smooth and graceful—until Pirouette landed with such a *thunk* that Shuffle lost her grip and tumbled into the grass.

Shuffle was sitting in one of Ever After High's beautifully landscaped gardens, far below the dormitory balconies. From the hedgehog's perspective, spring grass grew as far as her little eyes could see. Each blade reached taller than her head and smelled crisp and fresh. She nibbled. She munched. She ate until her swollen tummy stopped rumbling. Soon, all the sharp pains stopped and she felt good again. *What a relief!* She lay on her back, letting the sun warm her belly.

Pirouette's beak poked her. There was no time to nap. The swan cocked her head and pointed a wing at the far end of the garden. Shuffle scrambled onto her hind legs and peered over the tops of the grass. Lizzie and Duchess, mittens in hand, were hurrying toward the dormitory. Shuffle knew that if she wasn't in the room when Lizzie got back, Lizzie would worry about her.

Pirouette flattened against the ground and stretched out her wing. Shuffle quickly climbed aboard, settling onto the feathers. She gripped the ends of the ribbon, but she didn't close her eyes. This time she enjoyed the flight. The wind against her quills felt delightful. Far below, the students of Ever After High were going about their morning with no inkling that a hedgehog was flying overhead. Shuffle smiled so big the corners of her mouth started to hurt.

Through the dormitory window they glided. Pirouette landed atop her nest. She folded her wings and settled in. Shuffle let go of the ribbon. She put her fingers in her ears, expecting the hissy fit to begin as the swan protected her territory. But Pirouette scooted aside, making room for Shuffle's spiky little body. Shuffle couldn't believe it. She was sitting in Pirouette's precious nest. On her throne! She looked into the swan's black eyes. Without Pirouette's help, her stomach would still hurt. *How can I thank you?* Shuffle wondered. Then she looked down and saw what needed to be done. She reached her tiny hands between the reeds where peanut shells and corn kernels had become wedged, plucked them free, and tossed them onto the carpet. The swan nodded.

"I'm not mad at Ginger. I know she was just being nice," Lizzie said to Duchess as they hurried into the room. "She didn't know that Shuffle has a very delicate stomach."

"Those waffle thrones are so good I'd keep eating them until my stomach hurt, too," Duchess said.

Then both girls came to a dead stop in the middle of the room, their mouths hanging open as they stared at the nest. "Well, ruffle my feathers," Duchess said.

Lizzie was so shocked she dropped the mittens. "Shuffle? What in Ever After are you doing in that nest?"

Pirouette acted as if nothing was out of the ordinary. She preened her feathers as Shuffle grabbed the last peanut shell and threw it across the room.

"Are you feeling better?" Lizzie asked, kneeling beside the nest. She put an ear to Shuffle's belly. "You sound back to normal."

Shuffle grunted in her happy way.

"Well, I guess we don't have to go to Professor Poppa Bear after all. But I hope you learned your lesson, young lady. Next time, stick to hedgehog food. And that's an order!"

Shuffle turned up one side of her mouth in a mischievous smile. She reached out and patted Lizzie's shoulder.

"We'd better get to class," Duchess said. They grabbed their book bags.

As the bedroom door closed behind the girls, Shuffle yawned. It was daytime, after all, and she was overdue for her morning nap. Stretching her little arms, she looked for somewhere to burrow. Pirouette lifted her wing. Shuffle ducked beneath it and curled up into a ball. Who knew that feathers were so warm?

As she fell asleep, images of Wonderland filled her mind. The hedgerow, the roses, the sweet treats. Perhaps Lizzie was right and Shuffle should stick to bugs and Farmer-in-the-Dell granola. Perhaps she should never eat another waffle throne again. Never forever after.

Well, maybe just a crumb.

Or two.

Ginger Breadhouse and the

Candy Fish Wish

A Little ♡

Jelly Story

$\mathcal{O}$n an average school day at Ever After High, as students carried hextbooks and MirrorPads around campus, some also carried crates, cages, and leashes. Why? Because Ever After High was a very special place. Not only did it educate the sons and daughters of fairytale characters, but the headmaster allowed these sons and daughters to have pets.

We're not talking about ordinary pets like poodles, guinea pigs, or hamsters. Apple White, daughter of Snow White, had a lovely snow fox that curled up on her lap while she studied. Duchess Swan, daughter of the Swan Princess, had a trumpeter swan that slept in a nest next to her bed. Lizzie Hearts, daughter of the Queen of Hearts, had a hedgehog that burrowed beneath her blankets. Other pets included a phoenix, a unicorn, and a Pegasus. There was also a direwolf, a jackalope, and a dragon. Though it was possible to squeeze a dragon into one of the bedrooms, it wasn't advised. So while some of the pets lived in the dormitories, others were kept in the forest, the stable, or the nearby meadow.

These pets were close companions, lending a paw or claw from time to time to help students in their quest to fulfill their destinies. They were also reminders of home. Living in a boarding school had many benefits, like experiencing a new sense of independence, but homesickness was a feeling that struck every student at one time or another. So having a pet brought comfort.

Ginger Breadhouse, daughter of the Candy Witch, was one of the few students who didn't have a pet at Ever After High. She loved creatures. And she'd been homesick on a number of occasions, so it would have been nice to curl up with something fluffy and warm. But she'd never owned a pet. It wasn't because she had allergies or because she was too busy to take care of another being. In fact, soon after school started, she discovered a lovely little pet shop near campus called Farmer MacDonald's Menagerie, and she often visited. One day she sat on the floor with a new litter of direpups, inhaling their scent and giggling as they licked her face. On another day she fed peanuts to a flying squirrel. When a brown bunny with floppy ears needed a home, Ginger was tempted.

But Ginger had learned very early in childhood that no pet shop owner would sell her a living thing, out of fear that her mother would use the creature in a frightful recipe. The Candy Witch spent most of her time in her kitchen, concocting and cooking evil recipes. She kept a pantry stocked with all sorts of ingredients; some were plant-based, some mineral-based, but many came from animals, both magical and ordinary. She filled old spice jars with tarantula legs and worm casings. She kept tins of powdered unicorn horn and dragon scales. And no witch would be caught dead without a solid supply of eye of newt.

Ginger couldn't risk bringing home a pet only to have it end up in the pantry!

One day, after a stressful pop quiz in Science and Sorcery class, Ginger wandered through the pet store. She found herself standing in the fish section, where the aquariums were stacked ten tanks high. "The fish are so beautiful," she said to the shopkeeper. "So many colors."

"A fish seems a good choice for you," the man told her.

"Why?"

"Because you're as colorful as they are." He pointed to her outfit.

It was true. In her younger years, Ginger had dressed in ordinary, drab clothing so she wouldn't call attention to herself. She'd even tried to hide

her bright pink hair with a scarf. Her goal in those days had been to blend in and not be recognized as the daughter of the Candy Witch, because even a whispered mention of the word "witch" made people unnerved. But now, as a student at Ever After High, she'd come to realize that she was more than her legacy. She was her own person, and her passion was baking scrumptious treats, not wicked treats as her mother did. She began to dress the way that pleased her, adorning herself with cheerful colors, candy accents, and swirls, as if decorating a cake or cookie.

The fish seemed equally proud of their appearance. Some had neon splashes, while others were covered in polka dots. There were fish with tiger stripes, shimmering scales, and fantails. A few glowed in the dark.

"They're very easy to take care of," the shopkeeper explained. "All you need is a container of water and some fish food."

It was tempting, but Ginger knew that any fish she possessed might end up in her mother's bubbling cauldron.

And so the weeks passed at Ever After High. Ginger contented herself with her classwork and her baking. She started a MirrorCast show called *Spells Kitchen*. She enjoyed her classes and made new friends. But every so often that yearning for a pet would return. She would lie in bed at night and try to imagine a creature that would be safe from a witch's brew. But nothing came to mind. Still, that didn't keep her from wishing.

Then came a fateful evening. Dinner had concluded in the Castleteria—a hearty meal of beanstalk stew and hot cross buns. Rather than follow the other students back to the dormitory, Ginger decided to go to the Science and Sorcery classroom. Professor Rumpelstiltskin had been in an extra-grumpy mood that morning. Apparently, his boots were too tight, so in a fit of rage he gave all the students a fairy-fail on their lab work. Ginger figured that some hextra credit might help her grade.

By the time she opened the door to the classroom, evening had settled over the campus. She smiled when she found the room empty. The last thing she wanted was to listen to Professor Rumpelstiltskin holler and complain about his cramped toes. She turned on the lights, then flicked the switch on the fireplace. The dragon flame roared to life, spreading warmth over the counters and between the stools.

Ginger sat at her assigned work space and flipped through the Science and Sorcery hextbook. She decided to make a potion that was supposed to stretch leather. If she poured it on the professor's boots, he'd feel instant relief and maybe give her a good grade. It was worth a try.

So she set to work. She grabbed the necessary equipment—a miniature cauldron, a test tube, a dragon-flame-powered burner. The recipe was lengthy and complicated, so halfway through she pulled a pack of gummy candies from her book bag. Some were shaped like stars, some like worms, and some like fish. She set a handful of candies on the counter, munching one at a time while measuring ingredients. The sugar was just enough to give her the energy jolt she needed to focus on the task at hand. Things were going well. But then, as she was transferring the lime-green liquid from the test tube to the miniature cauldron, a noise sounded at the back of the room. Startled, she bumped her elbow against the cauldron, and its contents spilled.

"Sprinkles!" she exclaimed as she picked up her hextbook. The pages were soaked, and the potion was ruined. "What a royal pain."

"Hi, Ginger." Apple White entered the classroom. Her princess crown was perfectly perched atop her blond hair. "Have you seen Gala, my snow fox? I am fairy, fairy worried about her. She's not supposed to leave the dormitory."

A streak of white caught Ginger's eye. The fox darted beneath one of the stools. So *that* was the source of the mysterious noise.

"Oh, there you are," Apple said. She scooped the fox into her arms, then kissed her cheek. "Have you been hunting? You know that's against the rules. I do hope you didn't get into too much trouble." Apple hugged the fox to her chest, then smiled sweetly at Ginger. "You're so lucky you don't have to chase a pet around in the middle of the night. Well, it's getting late, and I never skip my beauty sleep. Charm you later." After a quick turn on her heels, she walked cheerfully away.

Ginger agreed with Apple's statement. How could she possibly add the responsibility of a pet when she had so many other things to do, like thronework and *Spells Kitchen*? But all she had to show for this evening's hard work was a big green mess. And she was too tired to start over.

After a long sigh, followed by an even longer yawn, she began to clean up. As she washed the cauldron in the sink, she noticed a little *tap tap* sound. Had the snow fox returned? She looked around, but nothing seemed out of the ordinary. As she washed the test tube, the sound grew louder.

Tap tap tap. What was that?

She whirled around. The noise was coming from her workstation. She wiped her hands dry, pushed her pink glasses up on her nose, and gazed across every inch of the counter. Over her hextbook and book bag, over the dragon-flame burner, then over a gummy fish that lay in a puddle of the spilled green potion.

Its tail was flapping against the counter. *Tap tap tap.*

Ginger was used to odd things. She'd grown up with a witch. And she inhabited a world where other students flew with fairy wings, where trolls worked the mail room, and where giants lived at the top of massive beanstalks.

But a candy fish flapping its tail was very unexpected.

"What in the ever after?" She picked it up so she could get a closer look. The yellow candy had a pair of candy eyes, and they looked directly at her. It also had a candy mouth, which opened and closed. It made a gasping sound, as if trying to breathe.

Ginger shivered with surprise. She dropped the candy and stepped back. The gummy fish began to flip-flop across the counter. A desperate look filled its bulging eyes, and the gasping grew louder. Then it flipped itself off the counter and landed on the floor, where it continued to appear as freaked out as Ginger felt.

The gummy fish was acting...like a fish out of water!

Ginger grabbed an empty cauldron, filled it from the tap, and then chased the flopping gummy across the floor. When the fish came to a dead end at the wall, she scooped it into her hand and dropped it into the water.

Never had she expected to see a piece of candy express joy! The fish smiled, then began to swim.

Around and around it went, its tail gliding from side to side. Ginger smiled, too. A moment earlier, the fish had been nothing more than a snack. But here it was, having the time of its life.

Life? Was it actually *alive*?

The curfew bell sounded. It was time for students to report to their dorm rooms and settle in for the night. Ginger didn't want to risk taking a cauldron from Professor Rumpelstiltskin's room. He liked to punish students by having them weave straw into gold. So she hurried down the hall and grabbed an empty jelly jar from the Cooking Class-ic Room. Then she transferred the gummy fish to its new container, flicked off the fireplace and lights, and carried the creature to the girls' dormitory.

"Want to see something weird?" Ginger asked as she burst into her bedroom. Her roommate, Melody Piper, daughter of the Pied Piper, was listening to music, as usual. She slid her earphones down around her neck.

"You got a pet fish?"

"No, not exactly." Ginger held the jar in front of Melody's face. "It's a piece of candy."

"Huh?"

"Look." She plucked the fish from the water and held it in her palm. Its tail began to flap. "It's a gummy fish. Lemon-flavored."

"But it's *moving*. And it has eyeballs." Melody cringed. "It's staring at me."

"Exactly." Ginger plopped it back into the water. Then she tried her best to explain. "I was eating candy and making a leather-stretching potion for hextra credit at the same time, and I was only halfway done when Apple's fox came into the room and made a noise. I was so startled, I spilled the potion on a gummy fish. *This* gummy fish." She pointed. "Then it started flapping around and looking at me." She took a huge breath of air. "I think it's alive!"

"It definitely looks alive." Melody laughed. "Hey, can you make other foods come to life?" She grabbed a banana off her desk. "A banana with eyeballs would be so totally wicked."

Ginger's mind raced. What if she could bring other foods to life? A cupcake that smiled or a peanut butter cup that danced. That would make a great episode for her MirrorCast show. "I don't have any more potion," she said. "I washed it all down the sink."

"Can you make more?"

Ginger shook her head. She'd been raised by an expert on wicked recipes and potions, so she knew that when accidental magic occurred, it could rarely be repeated. Not only were the specific ingredients involved, but also the temperature of the room and the time of day—even the cook's breath could have influenced the exact formula for the magic.

"Maybe this will be like Cinderella's pumpkin, and the gummy will return to normal at midnight," Melody suggested.

But it didn't.

The next morning, Ginger and Melody were surprised to see the gummy fish still swimming. "How come he's not dissolving?" Melody wondered. "He's made of sugar, right?"

Ginger shrugged. "That must be part of the magic."

For the next few days, Ginger kept the jelly jar on her desk. When she returned from her classes, she'd sit next to it and do her thronework. The fish would press his face against the glass and smile at her. She'd smile back. In the morning when Ginger awoke, she'd worry for a moment that the magic had stopped and that she'd find the piece of candy floating at the top of the jar. But each morning, he was swimming. She'd sigh with relief because, truth be told, she'd started to get used to the little guy. Her wish for a pet had come true. And he was the perfect pet because none of her mother's wicked recipes called for gummy fish!

Everyone came to see the little wonder. Some thought the fish was cute; some thought he was weird. "What are you going to name him?" Raven Queen, daughter of the Evil Queen, asked.

"Name him?" Ginger hadn't considered this possibility.

"He's your pet, isn't he?" Raven said. "You definitely need to give him a name. I named my dragon Nevermore."

"Well, he came from AA Candy Factory," Ginger said. "But that's not a very good name. Guess I'll have to think about it."

The next day, while Ginger was working on an essay for General Villainy, a tiny stream of water landed on her paper. A few droplets ran down the side of the jelly jar. *The fish must have been swimming too fast*, Ginger thought. She got a new piece of paper, but as she started writing again, a stream of water sprayed onto her nose. Ginger narrowed her eyes. The fish poked his head above the water's surface, aimed, and shot water out of his mouth, just like a hose. "Hey, you're doing that on purpose!" she said. "And you're making a huge mess!"

The fish inhaled a mouthful of water, then aimed again. A puddle landed on the paper.

"You're ruining my work!" Ginger cried. She placed a lid on the jar just as the fish was aiming for another attack.

The fish scowled, then turned away. Ginger tried to write, but she couldn't concentrate. Why was the gummy fish squirting water at her? Was he mad at her? Could a piece of candy feel anger? She tapped on the glass to get his attention. He ignored her. So she took off the lid, and the fish sprayed again. "What in Ever After is going on?" she asked as water dripped onto her shirt.

Since she'd never had a pet before, and since she had no idea why the fish was acting so rude, Ginger decided it was time to ask for advice. With the lid securely in place, she carried the jar down the hall to Apple White's room. "Come in," Apple called. She sat on a plush sofa, reading her Kingdom Management hextbook. Her snow fox lay curled up at her feet. "Oh, hi, Ginger. How's your fish?"

"I'm not sure. He seems kinda mad at me," Ginger explained. "He keeps spraying me with water."

"Oh, the poor little thing," Apple cooed, setting her book aside. "He's trying to get your attention. When Gala wants my attention, she chews up my pillows and shoes."

"What do you do?"

"I take her for a walk, of course." She pointed to a jewel-encrusted leash that hung from a hook. Then she reached down and patted Gala.

It sounded like good advice. Perhaps the fish was bored sitting in Ginger's room all day. How could she be sure? No one had written a book titled *How to Care for a Piece of Candy That Suddenly Comes to Life*. She'd already checked at the library. So Ginger carried the jar outside.

It was a perfectly lovely day, as it most often was at Ever After High. The sunshine was warm enough to open the flowers and get the birds singing, but it wasn't hot enough to cause unpleasant perspiration. Ginger held the jar aloft so the fish could get a good view. But he didn't seem interested in the trees, grass, or sky. He swam in a slow circle, a big frown on his yellow face.

A girl with lavender stripes in her hair was sitting at the edge of a pond, tossing bread crumbs to the ducks. Next to her, a beautiful trumpeter swan floated, preening her wings. The swan was named Pirouette, and the girl was her owner, Duchess. Since Duchess had a pet, maybe she could offer some advice.

"Hi, Duchess." Ginger sat next to her. The swan raised her head and stared at the fish with her black eyes.

"You'll probably want to keep your pet away from Pirouette," Duchess warned. "Fish are one of her favorite snacks."

"Oops." Ginger moved the jar out of the swan's view. Pirouette returned to preening.

"Do you *need* something?" Duchess asked. She sounded annoyed, but that was how she always sounded. Ginger had gotten used to her way of curling her upper lip in a slight sneer.

"I'm trying to figure out what's wrong with my fish. He keeps spitting water at me."

"That's rude." Duchess folded her arms and frowned. "He's probably trying to get your attention. When Pirouette wants to get my attention, she starts honking. It usually means she's hungry."

"Hungry?" Ginger adjusted her pink glasses. Could a candy fish be hungry? Funny, Ginger was all about food, but it had never occurred to her that a piece of candy would need to eat.

"I usually give Pirouette a bowl of green granola. She also loves lake grass and bread crumbs." She tossed a handful of crumbs at her swan. Pirouette stretched her long white neck and plucked them from the pond's surface.

Ginger thanked Duchess for the advice. She hurried to the Beast Training and Care classroom and found a packet of fish food on the shelf, next to a bag of unicorn treats. She carefully unscrewed the lid, then sprinkled a few flakes into the jar. The gummy fish swam to the surface and sniffed the flakes but didn't eat them. Then, before Ginger could react, he sprayed her right in the center of her forehead. Water ran down her nose and soaked her shirt. "Oh, you bad fish!"

She'd spent so many years wishing for a pet, only to realize that keeping one was a royal pain! But she couldn't get rid of the little creature. If she put him in one of the ponds, he would be eaten by a swan or a bird of prey.

She stomped out of the classroom and bumped right into Raven. "What's the matter?" Raven asked. "You seem out of sorts."

"Sorry," Ginger said. "I just don't know what to do with this fish. I've never had a pet before, and he keeps spraying water at me. I took him for a walk. And I tried feeding him. But he's still not happy."

Raven's dark eyes flashed, as if she understood. "I had a similar situation with my dragon when she first came to live with us at our castle. Only she wasn't spraying water—she was setting things on fire."

"That's terrible."

"One day she ignited all my thronework, and another time she incinerated my entire wardrobe!" Raven chuckled. "I tried giving her a time-out, but that didn't work. She set the time-out corner on fire."

"So you're saying that I just have to deal with this?" Would Ginger have to wear a snorkeling mask every time she sat next to her fish?

Raven took the jar from Ginger's hand and peered through the glass. The yellow fish stopped swimming and glared at Raven. "I tried and tried to tame Nevermore, but when she burned a huge hole through my bedroom wall, I thought I might have to return her to the wild. But then I talked to Ooglot, our family ogre. He told me that Nevermore was acting out because she was lonely."

"Lonely?"

"Yeah. She simply needed to spend time with other dragons. So I set up some playdates." She handed the jar back to Ginger.

Was it possible? Not only did the gummy fish think he was alive, but he also wanted to be with other fish? "I guess it would be lonely living by yourself in a jelly jar."

The next weekend, Ginger took a carriage ride to Farmer MacDonald's Menagerie. She showed her fish to the shopkeeper. "Sorry, but I don't have any fish like that one," he said with surprise. "I'd be happy to buy him from you. A fish like that could fetch a good price at market."

Ginger was tempted. The gummy was still glaring at her. She was getting pretty sick of his attitude. But she felt responsible. After all, she'd brought him to life. "I'd like to buy a couple of fish to keep him company."

"Well, big fish eat little fish, so you can't get a big fish. But these over here should do." He led her to the tank where some neon-colored fish swam. They were the exact same size as the gummy. "They won't grow much bigger, and they don't need much room."

She held the jelly jar close to the aquarium. The gummy fish pressed his nose against the glass, watching the other fish. He appeared interested, but Ginger couldn't tell if he was happy. Since taking the fish for a walk hadn't worked, and since trying to feed him hadn't worked, she didn't know what else to do. This was worth a try. "I'll take a blue one and a red one," she said.

"You'll need a bigger bowl." The shopkeeper took a round fishbowl off the shelf, then covered the bottom with brightly colored pebbles. He added two plants, a sparkly castle, and water. Then, using a little net, he caught the two fish and transferred them to the bowl. Ginger unscrewed the lid to the jelly jar and gently tipped her fish into the bowl.

She didn't know what to expect. Would he be upset? The gummy immediately swam alongside the red fish, then changed direction and swam alongside the blue fish. Then he darted to the surface and poked his yellow head out of the water. Ginger cringed, expecting a spout to hit her in the eye. But the gummy fish didn't spray her. And he didn't glare at her.

He smiled.

"Did your fish just *smile?*" the shopkeeper asked, scratching his bald head.

"Yep," Ginger said with a shrug. "I know. He's a really weird fish."

The three fish formed a line and swam through the castle's window and around the plants. "Looks like they're going to get along just fine," the man said. He handed Ginger a bag of fish food and rang up her purchase at the register.

Outside the shop, Ginger sat on a bench to wait for the carriage that would take her back to Ever After High. She set the bowl on her lap, watching as her pets enjoyed their new home. "Hey, you forgot this," the shopkeeper called. He stood in his doorway, waving the jelly jar.

"Thanks, but I don't need it," Ginger called back. Then she had an idea. She bent over the bowl and whispered, "I know what to call you. I'm going to call you Jelly. Is that okay with you?"

The gummy didn't spray her or frown at her. He paddled his little fins super fast, then rose to the surface and did a backflip. The other fish clapped their fins.

After all those years of wishing for a pet, it looked as if Ginger finally had one. Well, three, to be exact. And so what if they weren't cuddly like a snow fox or cute like a hedgehog? They belonged to her, and as long as she kept them at Ever After High, the new fish would be safe from her mom's pantry. And the candy fish would no longer be lonely.

"Jelly it is," she said. "Now, what should I name the other two?"

Hopper Croakington II
and the
Princely Present

A Little

Drake Story

*H*opper Croakington II, son of the famous Frog Prince, sat in the school's Castleteria, eating a bowl of curds and whey.

Actually, he wasn't eating. The spoon hung precariously from his fingers as he stared across the room at the princess table. His friend, Sparrow Hood, son of Robin Hood, was staring at the same table. "A pride of lions, a flock of geese…" Sparrow took a sip of hot cocoa. "What do we call a group of princesses?"

"Intimidating," Hopper murmured.

Sparrow snorted. "Speak for yourself, bro."

Because Hopper and Sparrow attended Ever After High, a boarding school for the sons and daughters of fairytale characters, they were used to eating meals with royalty and nonroyalty. Hopper should have been comfortable with the princesses. After all, he was a crown-wearing member of fairytale royalty. But when it came to talking to girls, Hopper always got a bit tongue-tied.

The princesses chatted loudly, their jeweled crowns gleaming beneath the Castleteria's chandeliers. While Sparrow went back to eating his breakfast, Hopper kept his gaze fixed upon one particular princess. Her name was Briar Beauty, daughter of Sleeping Beauty. She happened to be fast asleep, her head resting on the shoulder of the princess sitting next to her. She wasn't being rude. It wasn't her fault that she was asleep in the middle of a meal. Briar was cursed, and that was one of the reasons why Hopper had a mad crush on her.

You see, Hopper and Briar had two things in common—both were privileged enough to be born into royalty *and* both were under the control of unfortunate curses. Briar fell asleep at inopportune moments, and, at equally inopportune moments, Hopper turned into an amphibian.

A little green frog, to be exact.

Hopper sighed. Briar was the most amazing girl he'd ever met. Everyone called her "the life of the party" because she had so much energy. When awake, that is. Even though he wasn't a member of the Charming family, he often imagined that he would be the prince whose kiss would end Briar's sleeping curse. And he hoped she was destined to be the princess whose kiss would cure him of his slimy curse. It was possible. *Anything* was possible when you lived in a fairytale.

An elbow jab woke him from his daydream. "Your sleeve's in your curds," Sparrow pointed out.

"Oops." Hopper dabbed his velvet sleeve with a paper napkin. He usually took better care of his clothes. He couldn't control his transformation, but he could certainly control his wardrobe. He was quite fond of dapper velvet jackets, vests, bow ties, and loafers.

"Why don't you go talk to her," Sparrow said. "You want to serenade her? I just wrote a new song." He patted the guitar that hung from his shoulder, as it often did.

Hopper added sugar to his fairytale breakfast. Curds and whey was an acquired taste. "You know I can't talk to her."

"Oh right." Sparrow smiled slyly. "I almost forgot."

He hadn't forgotten. He was simply teasing his friend. The unfortunate fact was that each time Hopper tried to talk to Briar, he blushed. And whenever Hopper Croakington II blushed, he transformed.

To make matters worse, Briar didn't like frogs. She thought they were kind of gross.

"You want me to talk to her for you?" Sparrow offered.

"No way!" Hopper said. That would be totally humiliating. This wasn't spellementary school. Hopper Croakington II, crowned prince and record holder in the long jump, was perfectly capable of

asking a girl out. His heart began to pound. "She's waking up," he whispered.

Over at the princess table, Briar sat up straight. "What did I miss?" She rubbed her tired eyes, then pushed her long hair away from her face. "Even though I was asleep, I know you were talking about me."

"Of course we were talking about you, silly." Apple White, daughter of Snow White, put an arm around Briar and smiled. "We were planning your birthday party. We know how much you love a good party."

"What do you want for your birthday?" Ashlynn Ella, daughter of Cinderella, asked.

Sparrow elbowed Hopper again. "Did you hear that, dude? It's Briar's birthday."

"Shhh," Hopper told him. "I'm trying to listen." He leaned on the table, straining to hear. This was the kind of opportunity he'd dreamed about. If he could figure out what Briar wanted, he could buy her the perfect present. She'd be impressed *and* she'd notice him in a good way, for once.

Briar spread honey on a hot cross bun. "Seriously,

I have everything a princess needs. You don't need to get me anything. Being my best friends forever after is more than enough."

"But we have to bring presents," Apple insisted. "A birthday party isn't complete without them."

Briar took a huge bite, chewed, and swallowed. "Apple, really, you are so sweet. But I have an abundance of dresses, shoes, crownglasses, and drawers full of gift cards. I appreciate your persistence, but I mean it: There is nothing left that this queen-to-be needs."

"Then we'll have to find you something you don't have," Ashlynn said.

"Oh, this sounds like a challenge." Apple clapped her hands gleefully. "A shopping challenge! Let's go get a fableous present for Briar's birthday!"

Apple and the other princesses gathered their belongings, leaving Briar at the table. They hurried past Hopper and Sparrow. "Hi, boys," Apple said with a little wave.

"Hey, Apple," Sparrow said, waving back. But Hopper didn't say anything, because he was transfixed on Briar as she ate the last of her hot cross bun. After checking her MirrorPhone and sending a few hexts, she walked toward the exit.

"Here she comes," Sparrow said, punching Hopper's shoulder.

"I know, I know," Hopper told him between clenched teeth. "Stop hitting me already."

"Hey, Briar." Sparrow whipped his guitar onto his lap and strummed a few chords. "Hopper has something he wants to say to you."

"Really? What?" She stopped walking and looked right at Hopper. And that was all it took to turn Hopper's brain to mush.

"Uh…" Hopper froze. He didn't know what to say, so he delivered a corny pickup line. "Somebody better call security, 'cause my heart's been stolen." His voice cracked.

"Seriously?" Briar frowned. And kept looking right at him. "You said that to me last week."

And that's when the blush ignited in Hopper's cheeks.

Poof!

It was the sound he hated more than any other in the entire world. Because it meant that the curse had been activated and he'd been transformed.

Hopper had never gotten used to the sensation of finding himself in midair. Nor the feeling of falling to the ground and landing on four feet with suction-cup toes instead of two feet in nicely polished loafers. And then there was the whole size thing. As a boy, he never had to worry about being stepped on!

But he regained his composure quickly, stood on his hind feet, stretched his green body to make himself as tall as possible, and said, "Greetings to the fair Briar, whose name betrays her face, for no sharp point doth she possess, only softness and grace."

Yep, those words came out of his little froggy mouth. The other half of the curse was this—as a boy, he sounded like a complete dolt, but as a frog, he was masterfully poetic. He blinked his bulbous eyes at Briar, then spread his arms wide as if he had the leading role in a play and the lunch table was

his stage. "Give me one word of love, my darling, and I shall dedicate myself to you forever after."

"Oh, Hopper," she said with a sigh. "You're so weird sometimes." Then she headed out of the Castleteria.

"Weird?" Hopper whispered, his hand over his heart as if he'd been impaled by the word itself.

"Tough break," Sparrow said with a shrug.

As Briar disappeared from sight, Hopper's blush faded and he found himself standing on the table, back in human form. These changes in size were quite unsettling.

"Watch out!" a student grumbled.

"Sorry," Hopper said as he peeled a piece of toast off the bottom of his loafer. "Sorry," he told another student as he accidentally knocked over a glass of fairy-berry juice. He jumped onto the floor. Trying to regain his composure, he slicked back his hair, straightened his crown, and then strode out of the Castleteria.

"At least you tried," Sparrow said, following. "My old man tells me I should try harder at things, but you know how I feel about working."

Hopper frowned. "I try and I try and it never gets better. Briar thinks I'm weird. I don't know what to do."

"You could steal her—I mean, *get* her a birthday present," Sparrow suggested.

"But she said she has everything she needs. Besides, I wouldn't even know what to buy her." Surely Apple White and the other princesses would find something amazing for Briar. How could he compete?

But Hopper didn't want to miss out on this opportunity. After all, Briar's birthday came only once a year.

Even though Hopper didn't have a clue what to buy Briar, he knew someone who would.

If you're going to get advice on what to get a girl for her birthday, why not ask the most charming boy on campus? He would know just the right things to make a girl swoon. Lucky for Hopper, that boy just happened to be his roommate.

"I have no idea," Daring Charming, the son of King Charming, said. He lay on his bed, his hands clasped behind his head. "Girls always buy *me* presents. I like mirrors, shiny objects, and tanning lotions. You know, standard stuff. Oh, you can't go wrong if you buy me hair products. I love hair products." He opened his bedside drawer and pulled out a head shot. He kept stacks of them around the room. "Why not give her one of these? It's already signed."

"Uh, thanks," Hopper said. "But I don't think giving Briar a photo of *you* is going to get her to notice *me*."

"Oh, you want her to notice *you*." Daring sat up. "Why didn't you say so? Just say hello and smile at her." He demonstrated, and as he did, a blaze of light filled the room. How he kept his teeth so white was a Charming family secret. "It's easy."

There's nothing easy about saying hello, Hopper thought.

It was late afternoon, and the boys were hanging out, doing their thronework. Their room was opulently decorated with a chandelier, velvet and satin comforters, and royal crests hanging above each bed. Daring's side was full of trophies, his sword collection, and giant portraits of himself. Hopper's side also had trophies, plus his collection of jackets and vests, and a small photo of Briar taped to the wall.

"My mother once told me that girls like presents that come in small boxes," Daring said.

"Really?" Hopper recalled his mother saying the same thing. "So I should get her a piece of jewelry?"

"Why not? I once gave Apple a diamond-encrusted tiara. She loved it."

Tapping sounded at the window. A girl had climbed the trellis and was clinging to the vines, her face pressed against the glass. "Hi, Daring," she called. She waved, almost losing her balance. Another girl appeared. They were members of the Daring Charming Fan Club. "Did you forget about our meeting?"

"On my way, ladies," Daring said with a wave. The girls giggled and slid down the trellis. Daring stepped into his shoes and grabbed his letterman jacket. "Duty calls. Hey, do you have a fan club meeting tonight?"

Hopper sighed. "I don't have a fan club."

"Well, you should get one." Daring opened the door. Sounds of commotion flooded into the room. A group of girls had been waiting in the hallway. They began taking pictures with their Mirror-Phones.

"Excuse me," a voice loudly complained. Hopper knew Briar's voice by memory. He dashed to the doorway. Briar stood, hands on hips, a scowl on her beautiful face. "Daring, could you move your groupies? I need to get somewhere."

"Ladies," Daring said with a grand sweep of his arm. "Group photo?" He grabbed Briar by the sleeve and pulled her close. MirrorPhones clicked and flashed.

"Seriously, Daring, I'm late. Ginger's making me a birthday cake and she wants my input. I don't want to let her down." Briar pulled out of his grip. Then she glanced at Hopper. "And can you please tell your roommate that he shouldn't block the hall with his entourage?"

Hopper shuffled nervously in place. "H-h-he..." His voice cracked.

Poof!

"Your request, fair damsel, is but my command," Hopper the frog said with a bow.

"Thanks," Briar said. She slung her bag over her shoulder and disappeared around the corner.

Hopper hopped into his room and leaped to the window. He folded his skinny green legs and sat on the sill, peering through the glass. He waited patiently for a glimpse of Briar leaving the dormitory, but something else caught his eye.

A dragonfly walked along the edge of the windowsill. Hopper narrowed his eyes. A strange craving arose from deep in his stomach. In human form, he wouldn't have noticed the bluish-green insect, which was simply enjoying a bit of sunshine. But his froggy mouth began to water. "Worry not, little friend, for though I possess a rapier-like tongue, I use it for poetry, not the consumption of insects." The dragonfly did look deliciously fat and juicy, though.

It was difficult to control the urge. Hopper's tongue began to twitch. Just as it was about to unravel…

The dragonfly opened its mouth, and a long string of fire shot out, narrowly missing Hopper's head. "What in Ever After?" Hopper said with surprise. The dragonfly aimed and shot again. "My dear sir!" Hopper cried as a trail of smoke arose from the windowsill. "You have misunderstood my intentions. While I appear to be a frog, I can assure you that I am actually human. I do not eat—" Another string of fire shot out of the creature's mouth. This time Hopper had to jump off the sill to escape. He soared through the air, then landed on two human feet. The pocket of his velvet blazer was singed, but nothing else appeared damaged. He whipped around and stared at the dragonfly. "You breathe *fire*," he whispered.

While there were all sorts of amazing creatures at Ever After High, like a unicorn, a jackalope, and a Pegasus, only one was known to breathe fire—a dragon that belonged to Raven, daughter of the Evil Queen. Hopper had never seen a bug that could spout fire.

And it would fit nicely into a small box.

The insect flapped its transparent wings and flew across the room, landing on Hopper's pillow. He tried to grab it, but the dragonfly flew out of reach. He tried again, and again, knocking over a pile of head shots, a tube of hair gel, and two framed portraits. The dragonfly perched on the hilt of one of Daring's swords. With a sigh, Hopper sat on the edge of his bed. So much for getting Briar an amazing present. He hung his head. Maybe he'd have to give her the head shot of Daring after all. At least it was signed.

Zzzt.

The dragonfly landed on his sleeve. Hopper took a long, deep breath and kept as still as possible. The insect folded its back wings, then its front wings. After settling into a comfortable position, it looked right at Hopper. Hopper cringed. Was it going to set him on fire?

They sat like that for some time, neither moving. It seemed that they were sizing each other up. After a lot of awkward silence, Hopper decided to try talking to the little critter. "You probably saw that whole scene in the hallway." The dragonfly nodded. "She thinks I'm gross when I'm a frog. Just so you know, I wasn't going to eat you. I'm a prince. We don't eat bugs."

The dragonfly flew up to the ceiling and landed on the chandelier. "Oh, don't go," Hopper said. "I didn't mean to insult you. I'm sure bugs are tasty, but that doesn't mean I want to eat one." The dragonfly sat on one of the candles, peering down at Hopper.

Hopper leaned back against his pillows. "Briar's birthday is tomorrow, and I have no idea what to get her. She told Apple she has everything she needs. I wish I could just do something that would get her to notice me."

The dragonfly began to circle the chandelier. One by one, with its fiery breath, it lit each of the candles. A soft glow filled the dorm room. Then the dragonfly returned to Hopper's sleeve.

"Wow," Hopper said. "That was spelltacular."

Then he had an idea.

The next morning Hopper scrambled out of bed and began searching the room. He checked the windowsill, but there was no sign of the dragonfly. "Fairy-fail!"

"My thoughts exactly," Daring said. He stood in front of his mirror, combing his thick blond hair. "But there's no need for you to be upset. It's true that there's a pimple in the middle of my forehead, but I have the strength and courage to battle this enemy." He pulled a lock of hair so that it hung over the nearly invisible pustule.

"That's not why I said *fairy-fail*," Hopper grumbled. "I'm looking for a dragonfly that was in our room last night. Have you seen it?"

Daring wasn't listening. "Even those of us born with perfect heroic features must deal with a pimple now and then." He spritzed himself with his signature cologne. Then he slid into his letterman jacket and opened the bedroom door.

"Oh, poor Daring!" his groupies cried as he stepped into the hall.

"Fear not, ladies. My face will return to normal in a few days. Until then, we shall endure this hardship together." And off he strode.

Hardship? Hopper shook his head. He currently had a pimple on his chin, but no one was saying, "Oh, poor Hopper!"

As he dressed in his shorts, vest, velvet blazer, and loafers, Hopper wondered if there was still time to run into the Village of Book End and buy something for Briar. The signed photo of Daring lay on the nightstand. Surely he could do better than that.

Zzzzt.

The dragonfly landed on Hopper's sleeve. "There you are," he said with a smile. "I'm so glad to see you." The dragonfly wiggled its rump. Was it happy to see Hopper, too? "Remember how I said I needed a present for Briar? Would you help me?" The dragonfly nodded. It climbed up his sleeve and perched on Hopper's shoulder.

As quickly as he could, Hopper made his way out of the dormitory.

opper always sat at the same table in the Castleteria. Sparrow was already seated, chowing down on a platter of thronecakes and maple syrup. Hopper grabbed a muffin and a banana and slid onto the bench next to him.

The princesses were seated together, as usual. A colorful bouquet of balloons floated over Briar's head. She was dozing, facedown, on the table. Hopper nervously tapped his feet. Would he be able to pull this off?

"Dude, there's a bug on your shoulder," Sparrow said.

"I know. It's been hanging out with me."

"You mean, like a pet?"

"I guess so." He lowered his voice. "Anyway, it's my birthday present for Briar."

"You're going to give *that* to her?" Sparrow nearly choked on a bite of thronecake. "You can't be serious? Briar thinks *frogs* are gross. And you're going to give her a creepy-crawly insect? That's even worse."

"But it's not an ordinary insect." Hopper looked around to make sure no one was watching. Then he tore a small corner from his paper napkin. He held it up to the dragonfly. "Fire," Hopper said. The dragonfly opened its mouth, and the paper burst into flames. A tiny pile of ashes landed on the table.

"Whoa!" Sparrow said. "Hexcellent! But what if it sets her hair on fire? Or what if it melts her crown-glasses? She loves those things. I've never seen her without them."

Hopper was about to explain, when the giant mirror screen lit up. Headmaster Grimm's face appeared. Briar woke up, and like everyone else, turned to watch the morning announcements. "Good morning, Ever After High students. I have three important announcements. Firstly, today's forecast calls for a shower of rainbows, so if you find any pots of gold, please leave them for the leprechauns. Secondly, since many of you are at boarding school for the very first time, there will be a special lecture tonight in the Charmitorium on how to do your own laundry. And thirdly, let us wish an Ever After High happy birthday to Briar Beauty."

The Castleteria filled with applause. Ginger Breadhouse walked out of the kitchen, carrying a very tall cake. "One layer for each year of Briar's life," she announced as she set it on the table in front of Briar. Then she pressed birthday candles into the top. "Time to light the candles." She pulled a match and a flint from her apron pocket.

Hopper darted to his feet. This was it, the moment to strike!

"Wait!" he called. Everyone turned to look at him, including Briar. "I h-h-ha-" *Don't blush. Don't blush.* "I have a present for you."

Then he whispered to the dragonfly, "Go on." The dragonfly flew to the cake and, one by one, lit each candle with tiny fiery breaths. Everyone applauded again. Then a flurry of activity arose as the princesses whipped out their presents and crowded around Briar, blocking her from view.

"Open mine! Open mine!"

Had she noticed his gift? Hopper couldn't be sure. With a sigh, he sank to the bench.

"You tried," Sparrow said. They watched as wrapping paper and ribbons piled onto the floor of the princess table.

The dragonfly returned to Hopper's shoulder. "Well, Briar may not care, but at least you have the coolest pet at Ever After High," Sparrow said, trying to help Hopper feel better.

Hopper hadn't considered this. "Do I really have a pet?" He smiled. As he carefully patted the dragonfly's head, it nodded its head. "Well, then, I'd better give you a name."

"How about Dude?" Sparrow suggested. "That's a good name."

"Do you like Dude?" Hopper asked the little creature. It shook its head. "Hmmm. It's part dragon, so maybe I try a popular dragon name." Sparrow began to list all the dragon names he could think of. "Death-Horn. Firetongue. Night-Terror." The bug continued to shake its head.

"What about Drake?"

Startled, Hopper looked up into Briar's brown eyes. His heart nearly stopped beating.

"If you're looking for a dragon name, I've always liked Drake," she told him. The dragonfly began to hop up and down, nodding its head.

"Hey, looks like the little dude really likes that name," Sparrow said. "Drake the dragonfly. That's got a nice ring to it."

Hopper wanted to tell Briar that he also liked the name, but the words got stuck in his throat.

"Thank you," she said to him. "Sending Drake to light my birthday candles was a really spelltacular present."

She was thanking him?

"Everyone always gives me the same stuff." She held out a handful of gift cards. "But your present meant something. It was different and super-thoughtful."

"You're—you're—" He gulped. "You're welcome."

Poof!

As he landed on the table, on four suction-cup feet, Briar smiled at him, then went back to the princess table.

And for Hopper Croakington II, Briar's smile was a spelltacular present, too.

Dexter Charming and the Trouble with Jackalopes

A Little
Mr. Cottonhorn Story

$\mathcal{D}$exter Charming, son of King Charming, liked to study in the Common Room of his dormitory at Ever After High. It reminded him of the sitting room back at Charming Castle, where, until coming to this school, he'd spent most of his life. Stone arches graced the vaulted ceiling, and crystal chandeliers provided perfect light for reading. A fireplace offered warmth on cold days, and on warm days a cooling spell provided a steady breeze. And, just like at home,

mirrors were scattered over every inch of wall space. The main difference between the two rooms was that at Ever After High, a boarding school for the sons and daughters of fairytale characters, trees tended to grow inside, sometimes poking right through the roof. The Common Room's tree, a grand oak, was currently home to a pair of nesting starlings that screeched at students if they got too close.

Dexter made sure he was as far from the noisy nest as possible. He'd chosen an overstuffed chair in the corner, right next to a picture window that looked out upon the Enchanted Forest and surrounding countryside. He stretched his long legs, his high-top sneakers resting on an elaborately carved coffee table. His hands gripped a leather-bound volume of *Chemythstry for Beginners*, the required reading for his Chemythstry class. Though Dexter was a techie and spent a great deal of his time gaming on his computer, building robots, and attending Tech Club meetings, he still preferred reading from a page rather than a screen. So instead of crown-loading his hextbook onto his MirrorPad, as most students did, he'd checked the dusty old volume out from the library. Sometimes tradition was a burden, like when his parents expected him to fulfill his destiny as a hero, but sometimes it was a comfort, like the feel of an old-fashioned, printed book.

He turned the page, then pushed his tousled brown hair from his eyes. He'd already taken off his jacket and rolled up his shirtsleeves, but even though the fire wasn't lit, he felt too warm. After all, heat radiated from the furry creature who had wedged himself next to Dexter. The creature lay on his back, his long legs stretched to the end of the chair. A pair of black-rimmed glasses was perched on the creature's nose—the same style worn by Dexter—and he was also reading a book, which was propped on his furry belly. But his was not about chemythstry. It was an old tome about a lovely place called Mr. McGregor's garden.

In a nonfairytale world, it would be strange to see a rabbit reading a book. But this particular rabbit had been chosen for Dexter because of his keen intelligence. Over the years he'd picked up many skills, such as addition, subtraction, and reading. It would also be strange to note that a pair of antlers grew from the rabbit's head. To the students at Ever After High, however, this was a normal sight. Even the dragon flying past the window didn't cause anyone to raise an eyebrow. But the girl riding on the dragon's back had definitely caught Dexter's attention.

"There goes Raven," Dexter whispered as the dragon and rider swooped low, then disappeared from view. Mr. Cottonhorn, the jackalope, didn't much care about the girl. He preferred to focus on his book. The story about a garden filled with sweet peppers, tender turnips, and baby carrots was much more interesting than a girl with dark eyes and an evil destiny.

Dexter's stomach growled. He reached out and grabbed two thronecakes from a golden platter—one for himself and one for Mr. Cottonhorn. The creature's nose wiggled. Then he delicately nibbled the pastry with his big front teeth. Since becoming Dexter's official "pet," he'd developed a sophisticated taste for all things royal.

A few minutes later, their peaceful reading was interrupted as Raven Queen, daughter of the Evil Queen, stomped into the Common Room. "Ugh!" she exclaimed. Her long black hair was a windblown mess, and her spiderweb tights were torn.

Dexter closed his hextbook and scrambled to his feet. "Hi, Raven," he said with a shy grin. He adjusted his crown, for it had slid off kilter, as it tended to do. Then he glanced at the dirt stain on her cheek. "Are you okay?"

"I'm trying to train Nevermore to fly *above* the tree line, but every time she sees a sheep—*whoosh!*—she goes into a dive and almost kills me!" She eyed the thronecakes. "Near-death experiences make me famished!"

Dexter didn't know about such things. He'd lived a pretty comfortable life. And while his parents always encouraged him to be brave, he couldn't remember any near-death experiences. But it was quite possible that in his future role as a rescuer of damsels, he'd face dangers like the kind he always read about in graphic novels—teetering towers, sinister sorcerers, and dragons who weren't as nice as Nevermore. Time would certainly tell. "Would you like a piece of thronecake?" Dexter offered.

"Would I? You bet." Raven grabbed one. Then she plopped herself onto a couch. "I keep telling Nevermore that she can't go around stealing sheep. You're so lucky you have a jackalope who likes eating vegetables and livestock." Mr. Cottonhorn lowered his book and blinked at Raven over the rim of his glasses. "And he looks so cuddly. You can't cuddle with a dragon. Well, you can cuddle with Nevermore when she shrinks, but you have to be careful because her scales are as sharp as glass. And if she sneezes or coughs, she spouts fire, and that can burn your face right off." She reached out and patted Mr. Cottonhorn's head. "He's so soft, just like a bunny."

Dexter glanced at his companion. Mr. Cottonhorn was *not* a bunny. He was a jackalope, a unique creature who possessed superior jumping capabilities and a keen intellect. Along with reading, Mr. Cottonhorn could detect sounds from great distances and dig holes faster than any other creature at Ever After High. But Raven could have called Mr. Cottonhorn a hamster and Dexter wouldn't have corrected her. In his eyes, she could do no wrong.

He was smitten.

Raven was different. She was tall and skinny and often slouched in a way that wouldn't have been accepted in the Charming family. Her dark eyes and jet-black hair gave her a somber look, and the way she questioned tradition made her seem rebellious. It would have been easy to dismiss her as another brooding villain. But Dexter had discovered that

Raven was a constant surprise. He'd found her to be kind, empathetic, and often funny.

Mr. Cottonhorn suddenly sat upright and thumped his hind foot, a sign his kind used to signal that danger was lurking nearby. A large face was pressed against the Common Room's picture window. "Oh my wand!" Raven said. She wagged a finger at her dragon, whose wings flapped gracefully as she hovered outside. "Be careful with those wings. If you break another window, Headmaster Grimm will be furious."

Nevermore stared at the half-eaten piece of throncake. A little string of drool emerged from her mouth.

Raven shook her head. "No more sugar for you, Nevermore. You know it gives you a bellyache, and it's time for your nap." She pointed out the window, toward the forest.

Nevermore frowned, then turned and flew away. As she did, the tip of her wing knocked a brick loose, sending it tumbling to the courtyard below.

"Great. More damage. Last week she squished a

hedge. Yesterday she tried to swim in the unicorn fountain and broke it. And she's always stepping on the flowers or setting them on fire. Groundskeeper Green Thumb said that if my pet ruins one more plant, I'll get dungeon detention." Raven sighed. "What does he hexpect? Nevermore's as big as a house, and she shoots fire from her mouth. Groundskeeper Green Thumb probably wishes I'd received a kitten or a fish. Or a cute jackalope." She smiled at Mr. Cottonhorn. He ignored her—he'd gone back to looking at his book. "Hey, maybe we could trade," Raven said to Dexter.

Mr. Cottonhorn looked up and began thumping his hind leg again. Raven chuckled. "Don't worry. I'm just kidding. I wouldn't take you away from Dexter. Besides, that would probably mean breaking one of the headmaster's rules, and I've done enough of that lately." She ate the rest of her thronecake. "Well, I guess I'd better clean up that mess."

"I'll help," Dexter said. "Come on, Mr. Cotton-horn."

But Mr. Cottonhorn shook his head. Dexter glanced at the page. There was a drawing of a farmer with a rake, chasing a white rabbit. "Oh, I see why he doesn't want to stop reading. He's at the exciting part where Mr. McGregor chases Peter from the garden." Dexter began to follow Raven from the Common Room. "See ya later," he called.

Mr. Cottonhorn wiggled his nose.

The next afternoon, Dexter was in his room trying to memorize the periodic tables for chemythstry—H for hydrogen, CA for calcium, DR for dragoniun, and so on. Mr. Cottonhorn was sitting on the carpet, playing *Find the Carrot* on Dexter's MirrorPad. He'd just reached level six when someone knocked on the door.

"Hello," Raven said when Dexter opened the door.

"Uh, hi." Dexter's face got so hot his glasses fogged. Raven never visited his room. He immediately regretted that he hadn't made his bed and that he hadn't picked up the pile of dirty socks that was emitting a pungent odor. "What's up?" he asked, trying to sound nonchalant.

"I've got an idea I wanted to run by you. Can I come in?"

"Sure." Dexter quickly moved a stack of comic books so that Raven could sit in his desk chair.

"Well, the thing is, I've been having trouble with my spells."

"Really?" Dexter said, acting surprised even though he wasn't. Everyone at Ever After High was well aware that Raven's magic tended to backfire when she tried to use it for good. Her destiny, as daughter of the Evil Queen, was to wield powers beyond imagination, and using those powers for good went against tradition.

"I need to master my multiplication spell for Magicology. Everyone else is doing inanimate objects, like apples or tiaras. But I need to get a really good grade, since I've had so many backfiring spells lately. I thought I'd try to multiply a living creature. That's supposed to be really difficult." She looked down at Mr. Cottonhorn.

Dexter gulped. He'd do anything for Raven, but this didn't sound good. "You're going to *multiply* my jackalope? Mr. Cottonhorn looked up from the MirrorPad. His long ears twitched.

"Sure, I thought about multiplying Nevermore, but can you imagine the trouble that might cause? Raven raised her hands. "I haven't fully figured it out, but I think the spell goes something like… 'There's a little jackalope sitting on the floor. One is good, but I want one more.'" A blue flash erupted from Raven's outstretched fingers. "Uh-oh," she said. "That wasn't supposed to happen."

Dexter couldn't believe his eyes. "What the hex?" Mr. Cottonhorn started thumping his hind foot.

Dozens and dozens of little fluffballs had suddenly appeared. And each one had a tiny pair of antlers sprouting from its head.

"Why do I have such bad luck?" Raven asked, cradling an armload of baby jackalopes. "I wasn't trying to cast the spell. I was just trying to see if I could remember it. And I only wanted one more jackalope."

Dexter had counted thirty-five, but when he opened the closet, he found a dozen more fluffy creatures. And even more were hiding under the bed. Unlike Mr. Cottonhorn, who preferred his meals served on china plates with linen napkins, the little rascals began chewing on everything—computer wires, bedposts, and comic books.

"Where did I go wrong?" Raven wondered. "'There's a little jackalope sitting on the floor. One is good, but I want one more,'" she repeated, as if to herself, but a flash of blue lit up the room again.

"Oh no!" Dexter cried. His bed was covered with a new batch of babies. "Uh, Raven, could you please stop saying that spell?"

"I'm sorry. I was just trying to figure it out. It's only supposed to make one jackalope." She slumped into his desk chair. "Ugh! I'm so tired of my spells backfiring."

Mr. Cottonhorn began to hop in circles. He was not one bit pleased. He was a tidy creature who kept his nest clean and his carrots in a special basket. But these babies were causing a disaster. Some were digging holes in the bedding while others were gnawing the wood trim.

"Can you reverse the spell?" Dexter asked as he tried to save his comic books.

"What? I couldn't do that. Reversing the spell would mean..." She frowned. "It would mean making them *not* exist. That would be pure evil."

Dexter agreed. Even though the baby jackalopes were as destructive as a swarm of locusts, they were super cute. But all that eating meant a lot of pooping. His plush carpet looked as if it had been sprinkled with miniature troll chips! "What are we going to do with them?"

"I don't know." She petted one of the jackalopes that sat in her lap. "If Baba Yaga finds out I messed up another spell, I'll get a fairy-fail for sure."

Dexter wasn't just a prince. He was a Charming prince, which meant that one of his many purposes was to rescue helpless damsels. At least, that was what he'd always been told. And even though Raven never seemed helpless, at this moment she was technically a damsel. "When our cat had kittens, we put them in a basket and took them to the village and found people to adopt them," Dexter remembered. "We could do that."

"Oh, that's a great idea. Then no one has to know about my messed-up spell." She picked up a tan baby jackalope and pressed her nose against its wiggling nose. "Who can resist these things? They're adorable. I guess it's a good thing I didn't try to multiply my dragon."

"We'd better hurry, before someone else sees." Dexter grabbed a laundry basket, and they began to collect the mini jackalopes. But he could only find five. He looked around. "Wait a minute," he said. "What happened to the others?"

Mr. Cottonhorn stood in the doorway and pointed with his long ears. Raven had left the bedroom door open. A trail of destruction led down the hall and through the archway, into the Common Room, where the starlings had started squawking. Laundry basket in hand, Dexter hurried down the hall, Raven at his heels. Yes indeed, the jackalopes were hopping right through the Common Room. The two princesses who sat in front of the fire hadn't noticed the fluffballs. Apple White, daughter of Snow White, was busy hexting on her MirrorPhone, and Holly O'Hair, daughter of Rapunzel, was reading a book. A third princess, Briar Beauty, daughter of Sleeping Beauty, was taking a nap on the couch. The jackalopes disappeared down the stairway at the opposite end of the room.

Not wanting to draw attention to the situation, Dexter managed to tiptoe past, but Raven stepped on a squeaky floorboard. Apple glanced up. "Hi, Raven," she said in a chirpy way. "Hi, Dexter. I don't know why those birds are making so much noise. It's very distracting. I'm trying to have a conversation with Daring."

"It does seem distracting," Raven said, trying to block Apple's view of Dexter. The starling parents swooped at the laundry basket. Dexter batted them away as he headed for the stairs.

"Hey, look," Holly said. "Someone dropped troll chips on the floor." She reached down and picked one up. She inspected it, then flicked it away. "That is so not a troll chip. Gross!"

"Well, bye," Raven said.

"Charm you later," Apple called.

"That was close," Raven told Dexter as they bounded down the stairs. Mr. Cottonhorn took the lead, following the trail of chewed-up carpet and wood trim down one hall, then another. Then he skidded to a stop. A small hole had been chewed through one of the walls. It was the same size as a baby jackalope. Dexter handed the basket to Raven, then dropped to his knees. "Where does it go?" she asked.

He peered through the hole. The smell of dirt and manure filled his nostrils. "You're not going to like this," he told her. "But I think the hole leads to Groundskeeper Thumb's greenhouse."

Raven threw her hands in the air. "Oh no! First Nevermore sits on some flowers. And now I've unleashed a bunch of hungry baby jackalopes into his greenhouse. Poor Groundskeeper Thumb! He's going to be so upset. And I'll get dungeon detention for the rest of my life."

Dexter gulped. Was this his chance to be Raven's hero? He stood, repositioned his crown, and declared, "Not if we get there first!"

The greenhouse had been built along the school's southern wall, to allow for maximum sun exposure. A big sign on the door read:

NO RABBITS ALLOWED

Because Mr. Cottonhorn was not *technically* a rabbit, Dexter ignored the sign. He pushed open the glass door. A wave of humid air swept over them.

"Wow, it's warm in here," Raven said.

The greenhouse was made entirely of glass. Its ceiling reached five stories high, tall enough to fit a variety of fruit-bearing trees and vines. Butterflies flitted between sparkling flowers. Honeybees collected pollen for their hive, which conveniently dripped honey right into glass jars. And watermelons, root beer melons, and orangeade melons grew along trellises. Buckets, hoes, and rakes were set in the corner. A pair of gardening gloves lay on the ground.

"Looks like Thumb's not here," Dexter said, which was a huge relief. If the gardener didn't like rabbits, he certainly wouldn't like a bunch of baby jackalopes hopping around his garden.

The jackalopes had dug a tunnel under the glass wall and into the greenhouse, but the babies were nowhere to be seen. "Where are they?" Raven asked as she stepped beneath an arbor that was heavy with grapes. Mr. Cottonhorn stood on his hind legs, wiggled his nose, and pointed his ear at a sign that read:

VEGETABLE GARDEN

"Of course," Dexter said. "Jackalopes love vegetable gardens." Mr. Cottonhorn nodded and led the way down the path.

Groundskeeper Thumb had planted his vegetable garden in the back half of the greenhouse. Tidy rows, perfectly spaced and perfectly weed-free, lay along one side of the path. There was a row for cauliflower, one for turnips, and another for carrots. There were butter beans, string beans, and peppers in every color of the rainbow.

"Watch out for those snapping peas," Raven warned as one tried to bite her finger.

On the other side of the path, Groundskeeper Thumb had planted herbs in perfect symmetry. A little square of parsley, a bigger square of horseradish, a rectangle of dill weed. The garden looked like a patchwork quilt. Correction—it used to look like a patchwork quilt, but now it was covered in little fluffballs, who were eating everything in sight! They used their horns to uproot the herbs. Their sharp front teeth gnawed through the cauliflower.

"Whoops," Dexter said as the five jackalopes who'd been sitting in the laundry basket jumped out to join the others.

"Bad babies!" Raven cried. "This is an epic disaster."

"Catch them," Dexter said. Mr. Cottonhorn began running in a circle, trying to herd the jackalopes. But they refused to cooperate, hopping in every direction at once. "This is like trying to herd cats," Dexter realized. "Or worse! At least cats don't ram you with antlers!" The little jackalopes were using their antlers for self-defense, targeting Dexter's shins. "Ow!"

Raven plopped two squirming babies back into the laundry basket, but they jumped out as soon as she reached for another jackalope. "This is impossible," she said with a groan. "You should go before Thumb comes back. There's no reason for both of us to get dungeon detention."

Certainly, Dexter could have agreed. After all, his jackalope was a well-behaved individual who would never dig up someone else's garden. And Raven had been the one to cast the spell and stir up all the trouble. But Dexter couldn't just leave. Even though a Prince Charming was not destined to help an Evil Queen, Dexter would never abandon Raven in her time of need. He grabbed a wheelbarrow and began plucking the jackalopes from the carrot patch. Their little legs wiggled in protest. One gnawed on his finger. But he faced the same problem as Raven—as soon as he plopped the critters into the wheelbarrow, they jumped right out. "This isn't working. I need a lid or something." He found an old tarp and laid it over the top, leaving a small opening so he could continue to drop the jackalopes inside. Raven joined him. But as they chased the babies, they also made a mess, leaving footprints all over the soil. And when Dexter returned to the wheelbarrow, it was empty. They'd all escaped again!

"Ugh." He sat on an overturned bucket. "Maybe you should reverse the spell." Mr. Cottonhorn nodded, then shook the dirt off his fur.

"But that would be so mean," Raven said. "And besides, I'm not sure I can. Erasing spells are super advanced, and what if I erased the wrong things?"

Dexter shuddered. "Yeah, on second thought, don't do it. We'll just have to figure out a better way to catch them."

At that moment, a shadow fell over the garden. Mr. Cottonhorn looked out the far window. His hind leg began to thump. The baby jackalopes stopped eating. They looked up. Their hind legs began thumping. They were sounding the danger alarm, but what was frightening them?

"Nevermore?" Raven said. "What are you doing here?"

Nevermore, Raven's pet dragon, was sitting outside, staring through the glass with her piercing red eyes. Her gaze traveled up and down the vegetable rows. A little string of drool appeared at the corner of her mouth.

"Uh-oh," Raven said. "Dexter, I'm not sure if she's drooling over the veggies…or something else."

The babies and Mr. Cottonhorn started thumping louder and faster, as if they were forming a drum circle.

Nevermore pressed closer. The window creaked. "Oh no." Raven started waving her arms. "Don't lean on the glass! Be a nice dragon! Back away from the window!"

But Nevermore didn't go away. She licked her lips again, and in that instant, her razor-sharp teeth made an appearance.

The jackalopes began to run in tight circles, round and round, their eyes wide with fear. They bounded over Dexter's feet. "They're freaking out," he said, trying to grab them, but they were twirling way too fast, like little horned tornados.

"They're making an even bigger mess," Raven said as soil and upturned plants flew everywhere. "What can we do?"

Mr. Cottonhorn stopped thumping. He stood on his hind legs, wiggled his nose, and hopped into the wheelbarrow. Then he peeked out and made a soft squeaking sound. The babies stopped running in circles. They turned their antlered heads and looked at Mr. Cottonhorn. He squeaked again. One after another, they jumped in beside him and hid beneath the tarp.

"Brilliant!" Dexter said, proud of his pet for staying calm in the chaotic situation. "Good job, Mr. Cottonhorn." He grabbed the handles. "Now, let's get out of here before Groundskeeper Thumb shows up."

"But what about this mess?" Raven asked.

While Mr. Cottonhorn huddled with the still-trembling babies, Dexter and Raven raked the dirt to cover the holes and tidied the rows as best they could. But there was no way to cover up the fact that half the vegetables were currently being digested inside jackalope tummies. "You know," Dexter said, "it's risky, but you could cast that multiplication spell on the vegetables."

Raven furrowed her brow. "But my spells always go wrong."

"Just believe in your abilities," Dexter said. "You're destined to be a great sorceress, Raven. I think you can do it." He was entirely convinced, but then again, what could go wrong? You could never have too many carrots or turnips.

"Really? You think so?" She smiled. "You're always so nice to me, Dexter. How come?"

He could feel his face go red again. "Because..." Should he tell her how he felt? Should he tell her that if he could rewrite all the storybooks, he'd write a new one in which a Charming prince lived happily ever after with a sorceress? "I'm nice to you because you've always been nice to me." He smiled back.

Raven raised her hands and said, "'Little vegetables sitting on the floor. One is good, but I want many more.'" Blue light shot from her fingers.

ack outside, Raven patted her dragon's head. "Thank you, Nevermore. We couldn't have caught those babies without your help." She rewarded the dragon with a root beer melon. Then, with Raven and Mr. Cottonhorn leading the way, Dexter pushed the wheelbarrow down the lane toward the Village of Book End. The baby jackalopes, still upset by those sharp reptilian teeth, didn't dare stick their noses out. They huddled beneath the tarp.

Even though there were dozens of babies, it didn't take long to find good adoptive homes. Only someone born without a heart could resist the soft, cuddly fluffiness of a baby jackalope. By suppertime, Raven and Dexter and Mr. Cottonhorn were walking back up the lane with an empty wheelbarrow. "Thanks for helping me," Raven said.

"Anytime," Dexter told her. "But maybe you shouldn't try to multiply living creatures for Magicology."

"Agreed!"

Dexter, Raven, and Mr. Cottonhorn headed to the greenhouse to return the wheelbarrow and tarp. The greenhouse door was wide open. Groundskeeper Thumb stood inside, scratching his head and staring at the vegetable garden. So many vegetables had sprouted that the dirt was barely visible. "I can't believe it," he muttered. "I better use less fertilizer next time."

Raven and Dexter shared a quiet laugh. "I'm famished," she said. "Let's go eat." As they walked toward the Castleteria, Raven slipped her arm around Dexter's. "You know," she said, "I never thought two princes would come to my rescue." She smiled at Mr. Cottonhorn. Then she smiled at Dexter.

Mr. Cottonhorn bowed. Dexter's smile was so big it nearly knocked off his glasses.

It didn't surprise them that the Castleteria's special that night was vegetable soup.

Darling Charming and the Horse of a Different Color

A Little ♡

Sir Gallopad Story

*T*he stables at Ever After High, a boarding school for the sons and daughters of fairytale characters, were no ordinary stables. In fact, they were quite h*extra*ordinary, for they'd been designed to house a variety of magical creatures.

One entire wing of the facility had been built of stone and thickly coated with fire-repellent paint, in case a student needed to board a pet dragon. The unicorn stall was planted with thick vines and trees, since unicorns love to hide. The Pegasus stall was extra-wide, allowing for the stretching and

grooming of wings, and the griffin stall contained a perch and a large nest.

But not all the creatures that slept in the stables were magical. There were quite a few horses at Ever After High. All the King's Horses were the largest and most ill-tempered. They served All the King's Men, patrolling the campus at night to make sure students didn't try to sneak out. But of equal importance, they made sure no one tried to sneak in, like a village boy who'd been starstruck by Darling Charming's family fame, or an ogre who had a hankering for Hagatha's stone soup. All the King's Horses were black as night. They were respected *and* feared. No students were allowed to ride them.

The prettiest horses were reserved for the Princessology students. These gentle beasts were selected for their calm dispositions. Part of a princess's thronework was learning to groom her individual horse. Their manes were constantly being braided, dyed, and curled. It took a special type of horse to put up with that much fussing.

Then there were the horses ridden by the Hero Training students. They varied in shape, size, and personality but had one thing in common: strength. The horses had to gallop, jump, and swim across moats while carrying a rider heavy with armor.

Last, and certainly least, there were the oddballs. The misfits. The ones that didn't quite fit in but had somehow ended up at Ever After High. There was the mule that pulled Groundskeeper Green Thumb's cart, hauling weeds and delivering vegetables to the school's Castleteria. There was the donkey that gave rides to younger siblings when they came to visit, as well as the llama that basically just stood around and spat at passersby.

And then there was the horse who could change colors. Here's how he ended up at Ever After High.

Like most creatures that are lost and then found, the horse had a backstory that was short on joy and long on sorrow. He was born, as many horses are, in a barn on a farm. The farmers, Peter Pumpkin-Eater and his wife, Penelope Pumpkin-Eater, grew pumpkins, of course—some large enough to be hollowed out and lived in, and others of the perfect shape to be turned into coaches. The Pumpkin-Eaters required muscular draft horses to pull the plows in spring and haul the pumpkins to market in fall. After a year, it became clear that one particular foal wasn't going to grow as big as the others. He was not only a good head shorter but also skinnier than most, and thus wasn't cut out for pumpkin farming. And even though he possessed a beautiful coat of pure white hair, the Pumpkin-Eaters didn't want to keep him. "What good's a pretty horse if he can't do his share of work?" Peter asked as he nibbled on roasted pumpkin seeds.

"You got that right!" Penelope said as she sprayed whipped cream on a huge slice of pumpkin pie. So they hung a sign around the horse's neck that read RUNT FOR SALE, FIVE DOLLARS and tied him to the fence at the end of their long driveway. Then they hung a jar around his neck. "Have them put the money in this here jar," Penelope told the horse. They filled a bowl with water and another with oats, then left him there to wait. The horse ate all the oats and drank all the water. Then he wondered what would happen next.

Nothing much happened—at least, not right away. A butterfly landed on the horse's nose, then flew away. A pair of songbirds quarreled on a nearby branch. A beetle dug a hole in the dirt and disappeared. But no one came down the road, not even by pumpkin carriage. Hours passed. The day grew hot and the horse grew bored. He ate all the grass he could find, then began to nibble the vines that clung to the fence posts. And just when his eyelids began to feel heavy and he was about to lie down for a nap, he heard a sound—a chugging in the distance. He flicked his ears, then stomped one front hoof. Someone was coming! Would it be a new owner who would feed him lots of oats and let him run free in a field? He snorted with excitement.

The truck's brakes screeched as it stopped at the driveway. The driver's door opened, and a red fox in denim overalls stepped out. The horse watched curiously as the fox sauntered up to him.

"I do declare, it's mighty toasty out here." The fox pulled a handkerchief from his pocket and dabbed at his furry forehead.

The passenger door opened, and a cat hopped out. He was heavyset and was wearing the same kind of denim overalls. He also wore a pair of dark glasses. "Why'd we stop? Did ya find us a job?" He pulled a cane from the truck and tapped it on the ground as he walked.

"I stopped because I think I found us our next meal." The fox smiled slyly at the horse.

The cat smiled. His teeth appeared to be very sharp. "Is it a pigeon? Or a mouse? I love me a good mouse."

"No. It's a horse."

The cat stopped in his tracks. He tucked his cane under his arm. "I don't eat horse," he said with a scowl. "I got me a delicate palate."

The fox rolled his eyes. "The horse is not to eat, my dearest friend. The horse is to sell."

The cat, who was blind, ran his fingers along his whiskers. "Sell? But don't it belong to someone?"

"Indeed it does not." The fox tucked his handkerchief back into his pocket. "It is wearing a sign that says 'Free.'"

Even though the horse couldn't get a good look at the sign, he was pretty sure it didn't say FREE. Mrs. Pumpkin-Eater had said to put the money in the jar. The Pumpkin-Eaters never gave anything away.

The fox strode around the horse. "It's a runt, and a bit on the skinny side, but I'm certain it will fetch enough money to buy us a nice meal at that restaurant you like."

The cat clapped his paws. "Oooh, you mean the Bone and Gristle? I love that place." The fox untied the sign and the jar and tossed them aside. "Greetings to you, kind horse. I am Mr. Fox and this is my traveling companion, Mr. Cat. We are delighted to make your acquaintance." Though he was using very polite words, there was a wicked tone to the fox's voice, and it made the horse wary. He tried to step away. "There is no need to be afraid," the fox told him, with a sly look in his eyes. "Are you hungry, perchance?"

Was he hungry? The oats had run out hours ago, and the small patches of grass weren't doing much to fill his tummy. He nodded eagerly.

"Then, good sir, come with me and you shall be rewarded with some vittles." The fox untied the rope from the fence and started to lead the horse toward the truck.

With food on his mind, the horse followed the fox up a ramp and into the truck's bed. Once inside, the horse looked around. The truck bed was empty. No food. No water. He neighed and whipped around just as the back doors slammed shut, leaving him in total darkness. Then the truck's engine rumbled to life and the wheels began to roll. The horse's legs trembled with fear. Something was terribly wrong. Where were they taking him?

Up at the farmhouse, the Pumpkin-Eaters were too busy eating pumpkin pie to notice that their horse had been stolen.

*T*he ride was long and bumpy. The horse could hear the fox and the cat singing along to the radio. Then they started arguing about where they should sell their newly acquired property.

"I know a wicked witch who uses horse tails in her potions," the cat said. "And there are those two kids who keep tumbling down that hill. I bet they'd like a horse to carry their pail of water."

"While those are worthy suggestions, I have an idea that is much better," the fox said.

"Yeah, what is it?"

"Trust me. Have I ever led you astray?"

"Only on a daily basis," the cat said. Then the truck veered sharply to the left.

The horse, who'd never been anywhere but the Pumpkin-Eaters' farm, lay on the cold floor of the truck's bed and sighed. He wouldn't have minded carrying water for two clumsy kids, but he certainly didn't want to become a part of a witch's potion. He hoped this road would take him somewhere nice— or at least somewhere that had a full bowl of oats.

The horse awoke to the sound of the truck doors opening. He squinted as sunlight streamed in. "Come on," the cat said, yanking on the rope that was still tied around the horse's neck. The horse got to his hooves and walked down the ramp and into a place that was as different from the farm as oats are different from pumpkins. He blinked. Where was he?

A large, colorful tent stood before him. The banner above the entrance read:

THE PUPPETEER'S TRAVELING PUPPET SHOW

A line of parents and children stood at the ticket window. "Buy your tickets for the show," a man called as he walked through the crowd. "The puppets are so lifelike you'll think they're real!" Another man handed out balloons while a third sold root beer floats from a wheeled cart. The scent of buttered popcorn and cotton candy puffballs filled the horse's nostrils. His stomach growled.

The children all seemed excited for the show. Some squealed with happiness. Others ran in circles around their parents' legs. "Do not run," one of the mothers called to her daughter. "A Charming princess never runs. A Charming princess waits patiently." The little girl, who'd been chasing after two boys, returned to her mother's side in the line.

"What have we here?" An elderly man with a mop of silver hair approached. "That's a lovely little horse, Mr. Fox. Did you steal it?"

"Indeed I did not, Mr. Puppeteer," the fox said with a bow. "We have mended our old ways. This horse is rightfully ours."

"Rightfully ours," the cat said with a nod.

"However..." The fox flicked his long red tail. Then he pressed his paws together. "We do find ourselves in a bit of a financial predicament and could use some cash. We might be persuaded to part with this lovely beast, for the right price."

The Puppeteer stroked the horse's white mane. "He's a beauty, no doubt about it, but he needs fattening up. You haven't been feeding him enough."

"On account of our lack of funds," the fox said with a shrug.

The Puppeteer's smile set the horse at ease. "I could use him to pull the puppet wagon. And I'd better take him off your hands, just to make sure he's treated right." The Puppeteer pulled a well-worn leather wallet from his back pocket. After a quick round of negotiating, the puppet master handed the fox a crisp bill.

"We are most grateful," the fox said.

The cat licked his lips. "To the Bone and Gristle!" Then without further ado, the fox and the cat jumped back into their truck and drove away.

"Welcome to your new home," the Puppeteer said as he removed the rope from the horse's neck. The horse was grateful to be free of his captors. He bowed his head.

It turned out that the Puppeteer was a kindly old man. The horse ate well and fattened up in no time. Despite his small stature, he grew strong enough to pull the little puppet cart. The Puppeteer and his crew traveled from village to village, putting on puppet shows during the day and sleeping beneath the stars at night. It took only a few days for the horse to adjust to the nomadic lifestyle. And as long as his belly was full, he was content.

But a few years later in his career with the Puppeteer's Traveling Puppet Show, fate stepped in, as it tends to do, and everything changed.

On that particular, fateful night, the show was sold out. The tent echoed with laughter as people watched two puppets bonk each other over the heads with pie pans and rolling pins. The cotton candy maker couldn't spin fast enough to meet the demand,

and so much popcorn was spilled that it looked like a snowstorm. When the show was over, the horse stood next to his wagon. Kids huddled around, petting and hugging him. He always loved that part of the evening, especially licking the popcorn salt and caramel apple goo that lingered on their fingers.

"Well, I do declare." The horse looked up and saw a familiar face smirking at him. "I see you've been eating well," the Fox said.

"While we've been starving." The cat stood next to the fox. He was leaning on his cane. "That don't seem fair."

"Indeed it does not." The fox flicked his tail. "We found the horse this nice home, and now he's eating better than us." They did look a bit worse for wear. The fox's overalls had been patched at the knees, and the cat's were covered in stains. And both critters looked sorely in need of a good bath.

"Since we find ourselves short on cash, should we *acquire* him again?" the fox asked the cat.

"Sounds like a plan to me. Them trolls pay good money for horsemeat."

"Yes, they do. We'll wait until dark." After a wicked laugh, the fox and the cat got into their truck and drove away.

The horse had no way to tell the Puppeteer what had happened. That night, while the Puppeteer and his crew ate their supper inside the tent, the horse ate a bucket of alfalfa. The stars twinkled and the crickets sang, and after finishing his delicious meal, the horse settled on his bed of straw and closed his eyes for a nice sleep.

"Get up," a familiar voice whispered. A tugging sensation woke the horse. He darted to his hooves. The night was moonless, and a thick, pea soup fog had drifted in. Someone had tied a rope around his neck, and he was being pulled away from his straw bed. Whoever was pulling him was strong. As soon as he saw the truck's headlights, he knew that the fox and cat were trying to steal him again.

He neighed. He kicked. He bucked until he'd broken free of the rope. The cat tried to grab his mane. The fox tried to grab his tail. Panicked, the horse spun around twice, throwing the villains aside, then turned and galloped away as fast as he could. The cat jumped into the truck and followed. Headlights closed in. The road was no longer safe. Summoning all his strength and speed, the horse leaped over a drainage ditch and darted into the woods.

Some branches nearly tripped him, but he managed to charge deeper and deeper into the forest. As the headlights disappeared from view, the forest grew pitch black. The sound of the truck's engine faded. The horse leaned against a tree, trying to steady his breath. All he could hear was his own heart pounding. But it only took a few moments for that drumming to be interrupted by two voices.

"Where is he? Do you see him?"

"No. I don't see nothing but trees."

Two flashlight beams swept the forest. The horse didn't dare move, for a single step would draw attention. The beams swung left, then right, getting closer and closer. What could he do? His silky white hair would stand out in the darkness like a snowball in a sea of troll mud. He'd have to gallop again. But it was impossible to see. He'd be caught for sure.

The beams fell upon him. Oh no! This was it! He'd become the key ingredient in a witch's potion. Or stew for a troll family. But as soon as the beams had landed, they moved away. *I need to hide*, the horse thought. *I wish I could be invisible.*

"I still don't see nothing," the cat said. The flashlight beams swept over the horse again, but they didn't linger. "Nope, nothing there."

How can they not see me? the horse wondered. *They're looking right at me.*

"Drat!" complained the fox. "Well, I guess we'd better hit the road and find something else we can steal."

The horse waited until the truck had driven away and the headlights had faded. Except for a distant hooting owl, all was silent.

Exhausted and frightened, he collapsed to the forest floor.

———— ♥ ————

At sunrise, as the first rays of light filtered through the trees, the horse made his way out of the forest. Then, like a racehorse, he galloped down the road, eager to have his breakfast. But when he reached the field, his spirits sank. Everything had been packed up and carted away. The tent was gone, and so were the Puppeteer and his crew. *Why didn't they wait for me? Did they think I'd run away? Did they think I'd been stolen?* He snorted with frustration. Perhaps he could catch up with them. They'd be making their way to the next village. If he galloped as fast as he could, he'd surely reach them.

Down the road he charged, his white mane rippling, his hooves kicking up rocks and dust. He passed a sign that read:

VILLAGE OF BOOK END, 30 MILES ☞

That didn't seem too far. And if the Puppeteer wasn't there, then surely a nice villager would give him something to eat. But each time he heard an engine approaching, a shiver of fear darted down his spine and he dashed off the road, into the woods. What if the fox and cat drove this way, looking for him? The road suddenly felt too dangerous, so he decided to walk through the forest, keeping the road in view. When he grew thirsty, he followed his nose to a babbling brook. The water was crisp and clear. When his stomach began to rumble, he found a quiet grove where a deer had stopped to eat bark. The horse had never known that bark was edible. He tore a piece from a nearby tree. It tasted okay, but it was hard to swallow. He munched on some leaves, but they were bitter and stung his mouth. He searched for some grass, or perhaps a patch of moss. And that was when he realized that the road was no longer in view.

The horse was lost.

He hung his head, heavy with sadness. With a sigh, he sank to the forest floor.

How much time passed, he wasn't certain, but a little buzzing sound woke him from his daze. A small creature flew around his head, leaving a trail of blue-and-green glitter in the air. Wings flitted wildly as the insect zipped round and round. The horse had been stung by a bee once and he didn't want to repeat that incident, so he scrambled to his feet, ready to bolt deeper into the forest.

"What are you doing here?" The insect hovered in front of the horse's face. He cocked his head in wonder. The creature wasn't a bee after all, but a very small person with wings. She held a little mop in one hand and a tiny bucket in the other. "Shouldn't you be with the rest of the creatures? The ceremony is going to begin very soon."

What was she talking about? What other creatures? His ears flattened.

"Oh, don't be scared. How rude of me. My name is Viola. I'm a cleaning fairy. I work at the school." She pointed in the opposite direction. "It's a very nice place. You'll be very happy there, I promise. You'll have a stable to sleep in, and lots of good food to eat."

His ears perked up.

"You're a very pretty horse. One of the students is sure to love and adore you. Come on or you'll be late." She turned and flew out of the grove. "Follow me," she called.

*he horse followed the cleaning fairy to a meadow, where a crowd of creatures had gathered. "This is where I'll leave you," the fairy whispered in the horse's ear. "Wait for your instructions, and you'll soon be at the school." Specks of glitter fell onto the horse's nose as the fairy flew away. He sneezed. Some of the other creatures turned and looked at him. A small snow fox, who looked nothing like the wicked Mr. Fox, motioned for him to join her. So he did.

"Attention! Attention!" a voice commanded. Another fairy, this one much larger than the last, stood on a log and waved her arms. "Welcome to the Enchanted Forest. Not far from here, several students at Ever After High have gathered to receive their companion creatures. Each of you will be selected for a particular student. Your job will be to aid that student in the quest to fulfill his or her fairytale destiny." As she cleared her throat, a little puff of glitter floated from her mouth. "The ceremony will begin soon, and I need to make sure everyone is in attendance. Please make a sound when I call your name." She began to read from a clipboard. "Snow fox." The white fox tapped her paw on the ground. "Pegasus." A winged horse snorted. "Peacock." A bird stepped onto the log and began to strut around. Then his tail feathers opened into a glorious blue-and-green fan. The other animals applauded.

"Dragon," the fairy said. Branches cracked, and the forest floor trembled as a beast with scales stepped into the clearing. With eyes like red flames and smoke drifting from her nostrils, she was the most terrifying creature the horse had ever seen. With a shriek, he darted behind a tree.

I must hide, he thought.

"My, my, my," the fairy said as she flew over to the tree. "What have we here?" She hovered a few feet off the ground and spoke gently to the horse. "First of all, you have nothing to be afraid of. The dragon will not harm you. And second of all, are you aware that you are camouflaged?" She pointed to his leg.

The horse frowned. What was she talking about? He peered down at his front leg. It looked just like tree bark. His other leg did, too. His ears flattened again. What had happened to him?

"A horse who can change colors is very special and very rare indeed." She looked at her clipboard. "I don't see your name on the list, but I'm sure we'll find a match. There's bound to be a student who needs the ability to hide." She returned to her log.

Change colors? The horse couldn't believe it. Is that why the fox and cat hadn't been able to see him even though they'd shined their flashlights right at him? He'd wanted to hide, so he'd changed colors to blend in with the forest. Amazing! He stuck his front leg into a clump of tall daisies and thought about hiding. Sure enough, his leg turned green, with little white spots that looked exactly like the flowers. He neighed with delight. No one had ever called him *special* before.

"Excuse me." The fairy waved. "But we have business to attend to." Happy about his new discovery, the horse pranced back to the little snow fox. She smiled at him.

"Here's how the ceremony works," the fairy explained. "Each student has been given a popper that contains a magical spell. The spell will connect the student to his or her special creature. When the student pulls the popper, we will hear a snapping sound, and a bright light will appear in the sky. This means that the spell has been activated and that one of you will be magically drawn to that student.

It's as simple as that!" She flew above their heads. "Good luck, everyone."

To think that he'd been running for his life from two villains, had lost his way, and was about to meet a boy or a girl who would love and take care of him! The horse stomped in anticipation.

Snap! A flash of light filled the sky, followed by another *snap* and another light. "Oooh, those are the first two spell poppers," the fairy said. And right before their eyes, the snow fox and the peacock disappeared. The fairy clapped her hands. "This is so hexciting."

More snapping and more flashes, and one by one, a woodpecker, a direwolf pup, and a baby bear disappeared. Next went the unicorn, the Pegasus, and the jackalope. The dragon was the last to disappear, leaving the horse alone in the clearing.

"Oh dear, have you been forgotten?" the fairy wondered. "Well, your name wasn't on the list, after all. Perhaps you're not meant to be here. Maybe if you come back next year, there will be a match for you."

The horse hung his head. He'd come so close to having a real home. He turned away from the fairy so she couldn't see the tears pooling in his eyes.

Snap! The sky illuminated. And the ground gave way beneath the horse's hooves.

---

*H*e was standing in a different part of the forest. Girls and boys were laughing. A girl with thick curls was holding the baby bear. A boy with black-framed glasses was holding the jackalope. The dragon was being led away by a girl with jet-black hair and a shimmering black dress.

The horse perked up his ears. He'd made it. He'd been chosen. But for whom?

He looked around. Every creature had found a student. The peacock was walking next to a boy who wore a golden crown. And the snow fox had curled herself around the neck of a girl who also wore a crown.

And then he saw her, standing alone. Her hair as pale as moonlight, and her smile the sweetest he'd ever seen. "Hello," she said, holding out her palm. He sniffed her. Then he bowed his head. She ran her fingers through his mane. "My name's Darling Charming. I guess you're my horse now." She scratched his chin. "I wonder why you were chosen for me."

"I'll tell you why." The boy with the peacock walked up to them. He put an arm around the girl's shoulder. "He was chosen for you because he's on the small side. Mom and Dad wouldn't want you to ride a big horse. They'd be worried you might get hurt. This horse looks nice and safe." He gave her shoulder a squeeze. Then he and the peacock strutted away.

Darling rolled her eyes. "Safe," she grumbled. "I'm never allowed to do anything dangerous. Or hexciting." She cupped a hand around her mouth and whispered in the horse's ear. "But I have some se-crets. I'm not exactly as I appear." She winked. "What about you?"

He immediately turned the color of her blue-and-silver dress. She laughed. "I guess you're not exactly as you appear, either." While the other students left the clearing, Darling walked around the horse. "It's true what my brother said. My parents only want me riding gentle horses. And they prefer that I ride sidesaddle and wear a helmet." Then, even though no one else was around, she whispered in his ear again. "But what they don't know is that I love to go fast. Can you gallop?"

Could he gallop? *Like the wind!* he wanted to say. But instead, he nodded and stomped his front hoof.

"Really?" Darling looked around. Then, with a graceful jump, she pulled herself onto his back. Her fingers gripping his mane, she said, "They've all gone back to campus. No one will see us. Show me what you've got!"

And as they galloped out of the clearing and

through the nearby field, Darling Charming laughed with delight. "You *can* gallop!" she said.

After an exhilarating ride, Darling slid off the horse's back and wrapped her arms around his neck. "Thank you. That was the most fun I've had in a very long time." The horse felt the same way. His life thus far had been such a rocky journey, short on joy and long on sorrow. But as Darling led him toward the shiny Ever After High stables, he knew in his heart that his story had changed.

"I hope you don't mind if, on occasion, I ask you to use your camouflage skills." She giggled. "Just so we can have a fun adventure now and then." He nodded. She stopped walking and looked into his eyes. "And, because you're the horse of a princess, I think you should have the perfect knightly name. I shall hereby call you Sir Gallopad." She kissed both his cheeks, then bowed.

He smiled and bowed in return.

And his story began.

Apple White and the Snow Fox's First Winter

A Little

Gala Story

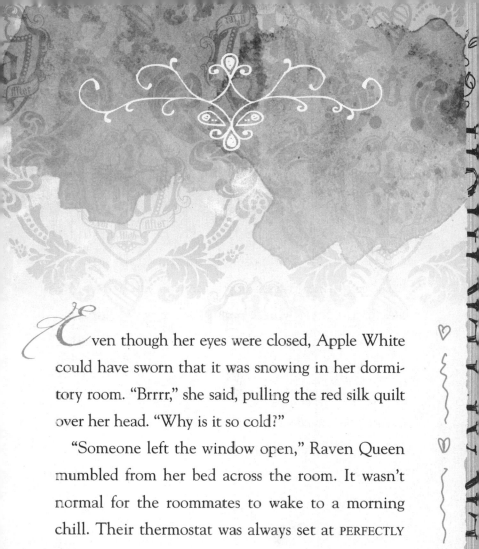

Even though her eyes were closed, Apple White could have sworn that it was snowing in her dormitory room. "Brrrr," she said, pulling the red silk quilt over her head. "Why is it so cold?"

"Someone left the window open," Raven Queen mumbled from her bed across the room. It wasn't normal for the roommates to wake to a morning chill. Their thermostat was always set at PERFECTLY PLEASANT.

"I'm fairy, fairy certain that I didn't do it," Apple said with a little shiver. She pulled her knees to her chest and tucked the hem of her cotton nightgown around her toes.

"I didn't do it, either," Raven insisted, wrapping her black-and-purple quilt around her shoulders. It was true that before going to bed, both girls had gone through their checklist. They'd looked under the beds and in the closets to make certain no wayward pixies had taken up residence. They'd set the alarms on their MirrorPhones so they wouldn't be late for class. And last but not least, they'd checked to make sure the windows were closed. This was extra important because if the windows were left open, a flock of songbirds would enter at dawn and chirp a happy morning song to Apple. Raven didn't mind pretty songs, but *that* much chatter *that* early could bring on a page-ripping headache.

The songbirds had, indeed, flown inside, but instead of singing, they began to peck at the thermostat, trying to warm the room for their beloved princesses.

"I could use some dragon breath right about now," Raven said. "That would make my bed nice and toasty."

"Wait a spell. If *we* didn't open the window, then who did?" Apple peered out from her quilt. A small shape sat on the windowsill. The shape was covered in white fur. "Gala?" Apple called. The snow fox's fur rippled in the breeze. "You shouldn't be sitting there. You'll catch a cold." Apple scrambled out of bed, grabbed the fox, and gently set the creature onto the bed. Then she hurriedly closed the window. The heating vents hummed to life, and warmth began to fill the room.

Apple climbed back into bed and hugged the snow fox. "Why did you open the window, you sweet girl? Too much cold air can make you sick." Gala looked at Apple with her little black eyes. Then she curled her tail around her nose and went to sleep. Apple had only known the fox for a short time. Gala had been chosen for Apple during a special ceremony in the Enchanted Forest, and Apple had been instantly delighted by the little fox. Such a sweet, affectionate pet for the girl who was known throughout all the kingdoms as the fairest in the land.

Raven, on the other hand, had received a purple-scaled dragon, the perfect pairing for the girl who was supposed to become the next Evil Queen.

One of the first things Apple did after meeting Gala was take a carriage ride to the local pet-supply store, Farmer MacDonald's Menagerie. There, she bought all sorts of supplies—a velvet pillow, a diamond-studded collar and leash, a pair of nail clippers, a porcelain brush, and a bag of fox kibble. She'd set the pillow on her bed so Gala could sleep next to her at night. It was nice having a pet who could stay in the dormitory. Raven's dragon, Nevermore, could shrink small enough to fit on Raven's bed, but even *small* dragon breath could set the whole place on fire. Being a fire hazard, Nevermore tended to sleep outside.

The MirrorPhone alarms rang. Apple yawned, then slipped out of bed. Raven did likewise. Their busy day had begun, and breakfast was the first stop.

Quick as a wink, the girls were dressed and heading for the school's Castleteria. To maintain a reputation as the fairest in the land, Apple always made sure to be on the cutting edge of the latest styles, and while she never wore anything made of *real* fur, she'd lately been seen around campus wearing a *living* fur. Gala loved to drape herself over Apple's shoulders, and Apple didn't mind one bit, except that the fur sometimes made her neck a bit itchy. But Apple loved her little snow fox so much she put up with the occasional discomfort.

Apple said her cheerful good-mornings to fellow students as she slid her tray along the counter. The porridge looked lumpy, as usual, but the fairyberry pancakes appeared edible. "Two pancakes, please."

Hagatha, the cook, flung them onto Apple's tray. "Ya want butter and syrup?"

"Yes, please." Apple held up her tray as a pat of butter flew through the air, along with a stream of syrup. Hagatha's manners were as coarse as her hair, which looked as if it had never been brushed. Apple thought about offering Hagatha some advice on hair care, but she didn't want to offend the old woman. The thick, wiry hair growing out of Hagatha's mole could use a nice pair of tweezers. Apple decided that she'd put *Buy Hagatha tweezers* on her list of Nice Things to Do. She kept the list next to her bed. "Thank you," she said. Then, carrying her tray, she chose her favorite table.

It was a typical breakfast. Apple sat with the other royal princesses, and they discussed everything from Kingdom Management thronework to Blondie Lockes's latest scoop to the girls' current crushes. Gala had already eaten a bowl of kibble, so she seemed content to lie next to Apple on the bench and nap. Like cats, snow foxes could sleep and sleep and sleep.

Spoons and forks clinked, and conversations bubbled. But just as Apple was finishing the last bite of pancake, a voice rang through the room.

"Rat!" Hagatha cried. Waving a spatula, she ran out from the kitchen. "There's a white rat in the walk-in!"

"Rat?" Raven said with a shrug. "What's the big deal? Rats aren't anything to be afraid of."

"What's a walk-in?" someone asked.

Ginger Breadhouse, who was sitting directly behind Apple, said loudly, "A walk-in is a refrigerator, but it's as big as a room." Being an expert on baking, Ginger knew all about professional kitchens. "It's where you keep all the perishables."

"That rat will eat all the curds and whey!" Hagatha cried

"Oh dear," Apple said. "Hagatha looks fairy, fairy upset." Indeed, the cook had climbed up onto the counter and was standing between the thronecakes and the gooseberry muffins.

"I hate rats!" Hagatha cried. "Dirty, vile creatures! Someone, go get Professor Pied Piper!"

"Do not worry, madam. I shall seek and find Professor Pied Piper!" Daring Charming jumped to his feet. Apple was not one bit surprised. Daring was very serious about his heroic duties. No damsel, be she a student princess or an apron-wearing cook, would go unaided in Daring's presence. As he ran out the Castleteria door, members of his fan club followed on his heels.

"Rats aren't vile," Ashlynn Ella said. She was sitting next to Apple. "They're actually very intelligent. I've spoken to many, and they are quite good conversationalists."

"I think foxes are also intelligent," Apple said. "Gala opened a window this morning. Wasn't that clever of her?" She reached down to stroke the fox but found an empty bench. "Where's Gala?"

Raven glanced around. "I don't know. I thought she was sleeping next to you."

"She was." Apple looked under the table. She looked under all the tables. "Gala?" she called worriedly. "Gala, where are you?"

Hagatha was still standing on the counter. "A kitchen can't have rats! The Fairytale Food and Potion Administration will close me down if they get wind of this. And this is the biggest white rat I've ever seen!"

Biggest white rat?

"Uh-oh," Apple said.

---

*H*er heels clicking on the floor, Apple hurried past Hagatha and into the kitchen. Steam poured out the belly of a stove while stew and porridge simmered on the burners. Flour, sugar, and piecrusts covered one counter, and chopped onions and turnips another. Apple darted around a basket of snails, then skidded to a stop. A door stood wide open. Cold air trickled out.

"Gala?" Apple called as she stepped into the walk-in.

Jugs of Farmer Brown's milk sat on shelves, along with golden goose eggs and blocks of butter. Because Gala was the only thing covered in fur, she looked totally out of place. She lay on a wheel of yellow cheese, her tail curled around her nose.

"Oh, there you are. How silly of you to sneak in here," Apple said. "You scared Hagatha half to death." It was so cold that Apple's jaw began to shiver, and the tip of her nose turned bright red. "Let's go."

Gala glanced at Apple, then slipped behind a vat of yak yogurt.

"Gala, you come back here," Apple said, trying to grab the fox. It took a few minutes of struggling— two wheels of blue cheese rolled across the floor, and curds and whey flew here and there—but finally

Apple caught her. "You shouldn't be in here," Apple whispered as she hugged Gala to her chest. "It's freezing. You'll catch a very bad cold." After a kiss on the nose, Apple wrapped Gala around her neck and walked quickly through the kitchen, passing Hagatha, Daring, and Professor Pied Piper, who'd brought his magic flute. "No need to worry," Apple reported. "The white rat is gone." She smiled sweetly. "Charm you later."

Apple carried Gala back to the dormitory room. "Now, you be a good girl." She set the snow fox on the velvet pillow. The fox's fur was still cold from her adventure in the walk-in, so Apple tucked a blanket around her. Then, after planting a little kiss on her head, Apple hurried to class.

It was late afternoon, and classes were over for the day. Apple and Briar Beauty had walked to the Village of Book End to treat themselves to something yummy. They sat on a bench beneath a weeping willow. The songbirds that often followed Apple were perched in the willow's branches, chirping their lovely melody. Apple sipped on an apple fizz she'd purchased from the Hocus Latte Café. Briar had chosen a mocha hocus latte.

"What the hex is going on over there?" Briar asked, peering over the top of her crownglasses.

Dexter Charming and Humphrey Dumpty stood on the other side of the cobblestone lane. They'd just ordered ice-cream cones from an ice-cream cart. A village boy had handed each prince a waffle cone with three scoops of ice cream. Dexter had taken a bite of his, then doubled over.

"Wh-wh-what is this?" Dexter complained. He stuck out his tongue.

Apple and Briar hurried to his side. "Are you sick?" Apple asked. Dexter didn't reply. He started to gag.

"Are you choking?" Briar grabbed Dexter around his middle, about to perform the Heimlich maneuver.

"No, I'm not choking," Dexter said, his tongue still sticking out, so it actually sounded like "Nuh, ah nah hoking." He picked something off his tongue. "There's fur in this ice cream!"

"But I don't sell furry ice cream," the village boy told them. "I've only got vanilla, chocolate, and charmberry."

"Then what's this?" Dexter asked, holding out a tuft of fur.

White fur.

Humphrey looked at his cone. "I don't see any fur on mine, but don't you think that looks like a paw print?"

"A paw print?" Apple stuck her face right up to Humphrey's ice cream. Sure enough, a perfect paw print sat in the middle of the top scoop. "Uh-oh." Apple whipped around. She stared at the cart. White fur. Paw print. "Gala?" she whispered. Then she lifted the cart's lid and looked inside. "Gala!" The snow fox was sleeping between a tub of vanilla and a tub of charmberry. Apple rolled up her silk

sleeves, then reached in and pulled the fox out of the cold and into the warm afternoon air. "What in Ever After is going on with you?" Apple asked. "You're beginning to worry me."

The fox wiggled, trying to get back into the ice-cream cart, but Apple held firm. "I'm royally sorry," she told the village boy. "I will pay for your damaged goods." She handed him the appropriate amount from her purse. Then she slumped onto the nearest bench.

"What's wrong?" Dexter asked.

"All day long Gala's been getting into mischief. Opening windows and making our room cold, napping in Hagatha's walk-in, and now leaving our dorm room and sleeping in the ice-cream cart. Why is she making so much mischief?"

Dexter dumped his ruined ice-cream cone into a garbage can. Then he slid his glasses up his nose and looked at the fox. "So you're saying that all day long your fox has been looking for cold places to sleep?"

"Yes. *Really* cold places." Apple stroked the fox's back. "She could get a chill and get sick."

Humphrey didn't seem to mind the paw print. He took a big bite from his cone, then did a search on his MirrorPhone. "It says on this MirrorSite that snow foxes have multilayered fur, a good supply of body fat, and special circulation in their paws to maintain optimal core temperature even in arctic conditions."

Apple's eyes widened. "Why, of course. Silly me. I've been worried about her catching a cold, but she's made for the cold. She's a *snow* fox."

Briar took a long sip from her hocus latte, then said, "Come to think of it, isn't it supposed to be winter right about now?"

Humphrey checked his phone again. "Wow, you're right. It's been so nice I forgot about the seasons."

Dexter scratched his head. "I wonder why winter hasn't arrived."

"Do you think Gala misses the snow?" Briar asked.

Apple pondered this for a moment. "But Gala was a baby when I got her. She's never seen snow. How would she know about it?"

"Must be instinct," Humphrey said.

"Yes. Instinct." Apple bolted to her feet. "Now I understand. Gala wasn't being bad. She simply wants winter." Apple draped Gala around her neck. She shivered a bit because the fox's belly was still cold from the ice-cream cart. Then Apple began to march up the lane.

"Where are you going?" Briar called.

"To get winter for my fox!"

With Gala draped over her shoulders, Apple climbed a steep spiral staircase, hurried past the Hall of Armor, then knocked on the massive oak door.

"Enter!" a voice bellowed. Apple opened the door and stepped into the headmaster's office.

Headmaster Grimm sat at his carved desk. His chair looked a bit like a throne, which seemed to befit a man of such authority. Bookshelves lined the walls, as did the heads of long-dead mythical creatures. The headmaster was dressed in his usual dapper clothing—a pressed dress shirt, wool waistcoat, and tailored trousers. Tall and broad-shouldered, he was an intimidating figure. Although he could be quite strict with students, he was always happy to see Apple. He motioned for her to sit.

"It's lovely to see you, Ms. White." He reached into a drawer, pulled out a thick file, and began to shuffle through the papers. "I assume you are here for a progress report. According to these records, you have been doing a hexcellent job as co-president of the Royal Student Council. Your grades are superb, teacher comments complimentary—though it does look as though you've been a bit tardy for Cooking Class-ic."

Apple frowned guiltily. That was her least favorite class.

The headmaster continued to peruse the file. "You get along with your roommate. You have not displayed any rebellious tendencies...." He folded his hands and smiled at her. "All in all, I would say that you are an exemplary student."

Apple was proud to hear such high praise, but there was another matter to attend to. "It has come to my attention, Headmaster, that winter is late."

He cleared his throat. "Did you say *winter* is late?"

"Yes." Apple peeled her fox from around her neck and set her onto the headmaster's desk. "This is my snow fox, Gala, and she's been looking for cold places to sleep. Humphrey just checked the calendar, and we realized that it's supposed to be cold outside." Gala stretched across the headmaster's papers and began to clean her front paws.

Headmaster Grimm looked at his desk calendar, then at his MirrorPad, then his MirrorPhone. "Ms. White, you are correct. Last week I hosted a series of fund-raising events for important alumni, and I wanted things to be perfect. So I put in a few phone calls to some friends and requested that they cast a

Fair Weather Spell on the school to keep winter at bay. Of course, the spell allowed for the occasional rain shower to benefit the flora. But we forgot to set an expiration date." He reached out and patted Gala's head. "Your fox is very clever. She has sensed that winter was supposed to be here by now."

"She *is* very clever," Apple agreed with a proud smile.

"I shall make a phone call and request winter be sent at once." He did so, and Apple waited patiently while pleasantries were exchanged. As soon as the call ended, the headmaster turned to the large mirror in his office and broadcast an announcement to the entire school. "Good afternoon," he said. Though Apple still sat in the office chair, she could hear the headmaster's voice echoing across campus as the Mirror Network showed his image on every mirror. "Winter will be arriving tomorrow at precisely seven AM. Dragon flames will be delivered to the dormitory fireplaces, along with extra blankets.

Tonight would be a good time to unpack your foul-weather clothing. Blizzards are to be expected."

Cheers erupted outside.

The headmaster frowned. "I trust I do not need to remind students that the Castleteria trays are not to be used as sleds."

"Did you hear that?" Apple asked as she hugged Gala to her chest. "Winter will be here tomorrow!"

The snow fox pressed her black nose against Apple's nose and smiled.

*T*he next morning, Apple was awakened by something pouncing on her bed. She opened her eyes to find Gala leaping back and forth between the windowsill and Apple's pillows.

"Wait till you see," Raven said. She was standing at the window.

Apple grabbed her robe, tied it around her waist, then stood next to Raven. "Wow!"

The campus had been transformed. Flakes were falling gently, coating everything in fluffy white. Gala darted to the door, then scratched at it. "She wants to go outside," Apple realized.

While Gala paced, trembling with anticipation, Apple and Raven got dressed as quickly as they could. "I used to love winter back home," Raven said as she slipped on a pair of boots. "Ooglot, our ogre, would drag a carpet down the hill, making the perfect sledding trail for us."

"I must admit, winter is not my favorite season." Apple pulled a second pair of wool socks onto her feet. She tied her boots, then buttoned her jacket all the way to her chin and stuck a fake-fur hat over her blond hair. "It's hard to walk in this many layers!"

As bundled as they could be, the girls waddled out of their room. Gala led the way, leaping and racing through the hall, soaring down the stairs as if in flight. "Where is she?" Apple asked when they got outside.

Raven pointed.

Gala was rolling in the snow. Sliding in the snow. Frolicking, bounding, and playing in the snow.

"Wow, she sure looks happy," Raven said.

"I guess a snow fox needs snow like a certain princess needs a poisoned apple," Apple said with a wink.

"Oh, don't get started on that again," Raven told her.

"Come on! Let's make snow fairies." Apple and Raven lay on their backs and moved their arms up and down. Gala pounced onto Apple's chest and delivered a big, wet nose kiss. There was no need to worry about Gala catching a cold. She was doing exactly what she was meant to do. And that was the perfect end to the story. Or, maybe, the perfect beginning.

"Happy first winter," Apple told her.

Narrator: As they say in the storytelling world, all good things must come to an end, and so, too, must this book. I hope you have enjoyed learning about some of the creatures who live at Ever After High. They are quite an interesting group, from a dragonfly who can spit fire to a jackalope who likes to read—and don't forget the horse who can change colors! Each and every one of them helps make Ever After High a truly spelltacular place.

Maddie: Uh, excuse me? Hello, Narrator. Aren't you forgetting someone?

Narrator: Hello, Maddie. Of course we didn't cover *all* the creatures. That would take many, many more pages, and the writer has other work to do.

Maddie: Yes, but I think there's one creature who's super special, and I'm sure the readers would love him as much as I love him.

Narrator: And who would that be?

Maddie: Why, my dormouse, of course, you silly. Would you tell a story about him? Please, please, please, with extra lumps of sugar on top and bottom? And in between? You don't have to worry—because he's a very tiny creature, his story won't take up much room.

Narrator: Well...

Maddie: Thank you! Did you hear that, Earl Grey? You're getting a story.

Earl Grey: *Squeak, squeak.*

Madeline Hatter

and the

Dapper Dormouse

A Little

Earl Grey Story

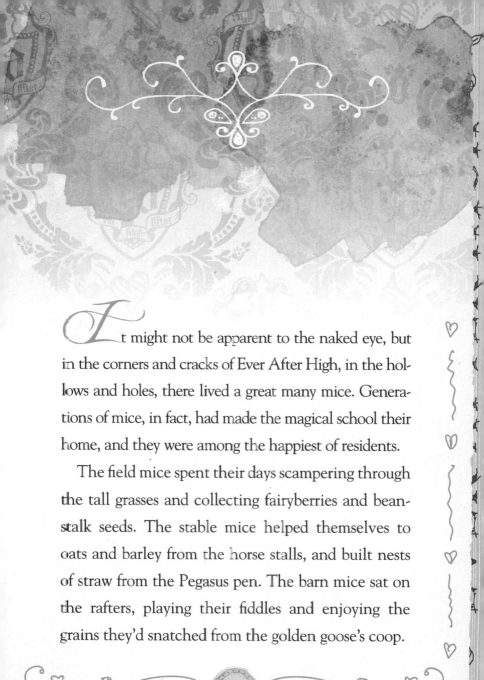

It might not be apparent to the naked eye, but in the corners and cracks of Ever After High, in the hollows and holes, there lived a great many mice. Generations of mice, in fact, had made the magical school their home, and they were among the happiest of residents.

The field mice spent their days scampering through the tall grasses and collecting fairyberries and beanstalk seeds. The stable mice helped themselves to oats and barley from the horse stalls, and built nests of straw from the Pegasus pen. The barn mice sat on the rafters, playing their fiddles and enjoying the grains they'd snatched from the golden goose's coop.

The pantry mice were the happiest of all because they spent their days sleeping and their nights gorging on a plentiful supply of delicacies. They were the plumpest of mice, roly-poly critters who slumbered in the pantry during the day, then awoke after the kitchen had closed. A lazy waddle beneath the Castleteria tables would yield a cornucopia of delights—thronecake crumbs, hot cross bun bits, and pieces of pickled-plum tart. The cleaning fairies were happy to let the pantry mice tidy the floor. That was so much easier than sweeping.

But there was one mouse who did not live among his kind—one mouse who spent most of his days and nights with a particular girl whom he loved with every cell of his tiny heart. His name was Earl Grey.

Earl Grey was a dormouse, small, gray in color, with soft, round ears and black eyes. He possessed the usual mouse-like qualities. He liked exploring, foraging, and eating. He enjoyed climbing, scurrying, and slumbering. But because he came from the faraway world known as Wonderland, he also

possessed qualities that were *unusual*, for in Wonderland, mice lived very different sorts of lives. It was a
place where nothing made sense and everything was
out of the ordinary, which was why Earl Grey liked
drinking tea and riding in flying teapots. He liked to
hum songs and solve riddles. And he loved wearing
hats and little gentlemanly outfits.

"What in Wonderland was that?" Madeline Hatter
asked as something bounced off her shoulder.

Maddie, who was also from Wonderland and who
happened to be the daughter of the famously odd
Mad Hatter, was walking with her friend Raven
Queen. Maddie was wearing her favorite teacup-
shaped hat and a lovely flouncy dress that was both
checkered and striped. Blue polka-dot tights and a
bright blue bow completed the adorable outfit.
Raven wore a black dress with spiderweb-detailed
tights. The two girls looked as different as day and
night.

"I think Earl Grey just threw his boot," Raven
said. Raven pointed to Maddie's hat. Earl Grey had

been riding on the brim, but now he was hiding in-side the hat. The girls stopped walking.

"But this is a Thursday, and boot-throwing is usu-ally reserved for days that are other than Thursday," Maddie said. "At least, I believe that is true, and so it must be, for what we believe is more true than anything else."

Raven couldn't help smiling. She'd been friends with Maddie for a while now, so she was used to this sort of explanation. Another boot flew out of Mad-die's hat. Raven caught the second boot just before it hit her. "Yep, he's throwing his boots."

"Oh, how cute," Maddie said. "Should we throw our shoes?" She slipped out of her purple shoes and flung them into a hedge. Raven, however, held the little mouse boot close to her face and narrowed her eyes.

"It's awfully small," Raven said, "but it looks like there's a hole in the sole."

"Is that a riddle?" Maddie asked, clapping her hands. "I've never heard that one. Let me guess. You know how much I love riddles."

"It's not a riddle," Raven told her. "There is *literally* a hole in this boot's sole." She handed it to Maddie.

Maddie examined the boot, then frowned. "Oh dear, there is a hole. Poor little Earl Grey. His little toes could have caught a cold."

Earl Grey's furry face peeked over the brim of Maddie's teacup hat. He wiggled his nose. While some students might have found it odd to walk around with a dormouse on their heads, Maddie found it quite normal. Everyone on campus knew that Maddie's dormouse liked to ride inside her hat. And why not? It was a perfect travel arrangement. The hat offered Earl Grey a comfortable seat where he could watch the world go by, safe from prowling cats. And if a hungry dragon flew overhead, he could hunker down and disappear from view.

Earl Gray squeaked, then threw something else. Raven caught it. "It's his vest," she said. Then he threw out his tiny top hat. "Why is your pet taking off his clothes?"

"Well, what other choice does he have? He certainly can't put them *on* if they're already on," Maddie said matter-of-factly.

"He seems upset." Raven looked at Maddie's hat. The dormouse was shaking his fists in the air. "I think he's having a tantrum."

"How hextremely bewildering," Maddie said. "I don't know what he'd be tantrumming about. I spritzed him with his favorite mousey cologne, Eau de Fromage. And I fed him his favorite cheese-flavored cereal for breakfast." While Maddie was quite skilled at interpreting her pet's emotions, he'd never thrown a boot at her before. "I wish I knew how to speak Mouse."

"Ashlynn knows."

"Oh, Raven, what a spelltacular idea." Maddie hugged her friend. "Let's go find Ashlynn."

Ashlynn Ella, daughter of Cinderella, had a special gift. She was able to speak many different animal languages. Hopefully, she'd be able to understand the squeaking and grumbling coming from Maddie's hat.

Maddie and Raven found Ashlynn standing beneath a tree in one of Ever After High's beautiful gardens. "Hi, Ashlynn," Maddie called as she and Raven approached.

"Hi," Ashlynn said. She looked at Maddie's feet. "Why are you barefoot?"

"I threw my shoes. Apparently it's shoe-throwing day," Maddie told her with a shrug. "So anyhoo, are you busy? I need your help."

"I would love to help you, but I am actually a little busy! There's a nest of pigeons in this tree, and this little critter fell out." She opened her hands, in which she was cradling a baby bird.

"Oh, it's so cute," Raven said.

"It was trying to fly much too early," Ashlynn explained. "The mother bird is very upset." A full-grown pigeon was circling above the girls' heads, making a horrid racket. Ashlynn looked up at the bird. The mama bird stopped squawking and settled on a branch next to her nest. "I told her not to worry. Help is on the way."

"What kind of help?" Maddie asked.

Ashlynn smiled. "Here it comes now."

A white swan waddled up to them. It was Pirouette, Duchess Swan's pet. Ashlynn talked to her. The swan nodded and opened her beak. Ashlynn gently placed the baby bird into the open beak. Then the swan flew up to the nest and set the bird next to its siblings. Ashlynn thanked Pirouette. The swan honked back, then flew away. The baby bird opened its mouth, and its mama began to feed it.

"That was fableous, Ashlynn," Raven said.

"Thanks. I do my best." Ashlynn pushed a strand of golden hair from her eyes. "So, what kind of help do you need?"

Maddie pointed to her hat. "Can you please speak to my mousey? I don't understand what he wants. He took off his boots, vest, and hat and threw them at us."

"Well, that seems odd," Ashlynn said. She tried

talking to Earl Grey. Earl Grey poked his head out of the hat and squeaked back.

"What's he saying?" Maddie asked.

"Well, it's a bit jumbled," Ashlynn told her. "Riddlish is very confusing, and it's extra confusing in Mouse. He said something like…'The cupboard can be bare, but the thread should not be.'"

"Riddlish is pretty confusing," Raven said. "Whether or not it's in Mouse."

"'The cupboard can be bare, but the thread should not be.'" Maddie bounced on her toes. "Oh, I know the answer. The thread should not be bare. His clothes are threadbare. They're old. He wants new clothes!" Then she inspected the little vest. "Why, it's true," she agreed. "And the seams are coming apart." She looked at the hat. "The brim is stretched and loose." She stuck the dormouse's clothes into one of her many pockets. Then she reached her hand up to her hat, waiting for Earl Grey to climb onto her palm. Once she felt his tiny paws against her skin, she lowered her hand and looked into his black eyes. "My sweet Sir Mousey," she said to him. "Do not despair."

Earl Grey's whiskers twitched, and he hung his head. The truth was, without his hat, boots, or vest, Earl Grey looked like an ordinary mouse. And that was no good!

"We will find you a new set of clothes, and you will look as dapper as ever," Maddie said. Earl Grey smiled and clapped his paws.

"Where will you get new clothes?" Raven asked.

"When *where* and *ever* get together, then that is the very place," Maddie said.

Raven scratched her head. "Wherever?"

"Hexactly so! And the best wherever I know is my dad's shop."

"Oh, that's a good idea. You can ask him for a mouse-sized hat," Ashlynn said.

Maddie smiled. "Or we can *not* ask him. For he never knows the answer, so if we don't ask the question, then everything will work out fine."

Earl Grey nodded. Maddie set him back into the teacup hat. Raven shrugged. "That makes about as much sense as my Chemythstry thronework. But I guess I'll join you. I could use a cup of tea."

"Would you like to come, too?" Maddie asked Ashlynn.

"I'd love to, but I'm supposed to be at the Glass Slipper in five minutes for my shift. Come by later, and we'll pick out a new pair of shoes for you," she told Maddie. Then Ashlynn checked her Mirror-Phone. "Uh-oh, I'd better hurry. You know what happens if I'm late!" She ran off.

"What happens if she's late?" Maddie asked Raven.

"Her clothes turn to rags. It's part of her destiny. When the clock strikes midnight, her clothes turn back, and the coach becomes a pumpkin, and the footmen become lizards. Remember?"

Maddie scrunched up her face, then giggled. "And you think I'm the one who doesn't make sense." Earl Grey squeaked in agreement.

With Earl Grey sitting in her hat and Raven walking beside her, Maddie followed the winding lane to the Village of Book End. Luckily, the cobblestones were smooth on her feet. She wiggled her toes. "I love walking barefoot," she said. "I think I'll do it more often!" Earl Grey didn't seem to mind Maddie's bouncy steps. He held tight to the teacup hat, his whiskers twitching in the breeze. "In Wonderland, we'd have no trouble finding Earl Grey some new clothes, because there's a store just for mice," Maddie said dreamily. She loved talking about her home. "I couldn't fit inside, of course, unless I took a shrinking potion. But if I stretched out on my belly, I could look through the teeny-tiny window."

"Who makes the mouse clothes?" Raven asked.

"The mice do, of course. Wonderland mice are tea-riffic with needles and thread. They make hats with ear holes, and trousers with tail holes. Vests with upside-down pockets, and boots with buttons.

And special mouse-sized sunglasses for moonlight. And umbrellas. Lots and lots of umbrellas."

"Why umbrellas?" Raven asked.

"Umbrellas are a very important mouse accessory. Think about it: A single raindrop on a mouse's head is like a bucket of water on a person's head." Maddie skidded to a stop. "Oh, here we are." They stood outside the Mad Hatter of Wonderland's Haberdashery and Tea Shoppe. The window display was a confusing jumble of tea tins and teacups, hats filled with tea bags, teapots shaped like hats, and hats shaped like teapots.

Raven pointed to a sign that was taped to the door:

NO ROOM, NO ROOM

"Uh, it looks like the place is full. Maybe we should come back another time."

"There is no other time better than the present time," Maddie said. "That's why they call it the *present*. Get it? Because it's like a *present*."

"I've actually heard that one," Raven said, grinning.

"Then let's open it!" And with a grand sweep of her arms, Maddie opened the door, and she and Raven stepped inside.

Though Maddie was a naturally cheerful person, her happiness registered off the meter whenever she entered her father's shop. Other than the Wonderland Grove, the shop was the only place at Ever After High that was one thousand and two percent Wonderland. Cups and saucers were stacked all the way to the ceiling, and though the piles tilted precariously, they did not fall over. Chairs tapped their feet to the jazzy music playing on an old-fashioned radio. Usually, butter knives and teaspoons flew around, making sure no cup of tea went unbuttered and no scone went unstirred. On this particular afternoon, however, there were no other customers, so the butter knives and teaspoons were taking naps.

"Bottom of the morning to you," a voice called. The Mad Hatter, dressed in his usual array of bold colors and prints, bounded from the back room. He swept his daughter into a hug and swung her around in a circle. Then he took off his top hat and bowed to Raven. "Your Majesty," he said.

Raven blushed. She returned the bow. "Your Highness."

Ever so delicately, the Mad Hatter shook Earl Grey's paw. "Your Mousiness." Earl Grey squeaked. Then the little critter climbed out of the teacup hat, scurried down Maddie's arm, and leaped onto a table. "Hellooo. What in the wonderlandiful world is this?" the Mad Hatter said. "Your pet is wearing nothing but fur."

Maddie giggled. "He took off all his clothes and threw them at us."

"How delightful," the Mad Hatter said. "What a bold and perfectly mousey move!"

"Dad, do you have any hats that might fit Earl Grey?"

"Do I? I thought you'd never ask." The Mad Hatter grabbed a bowler hat from a hook and placed it over the creature. "A hat to hide in." He grabbed a flying hat and set Earl Grey inside. "A hat to ride in." He plucked the dormouse out of the air and stuck him on a shelf, next to a cupcake hat. "A hat that's sweet." Then the Mad Hatter stuck his own foot into a shoe-shaped hat. "A hat for feet."

Raven laughed. "Isn't a hat for feet actually a shoe?"

"Nonsense," the Mad Hatter said. "That would be like saying a shirt for legs is actually a pair of pants."

Raven shrugged. How could a person argue with that kind of logic?

Maddie looked around the room. She spied a tiny hat rack tucked beneath a larger hat rack. "Oh, how tea-riffic," she said as she knelt to inspect the hats. They were clearly meant for smaller critters. Each hat had ear holes. One hat seemed perfect for a rabbit, and a few seemed the right size for squirrels. "I think this one will do." She selected a black top hat. Earl Grey scampered down the shelves and leaped onto a table. Maddie set the hat on his head.

"That looks great," Raven said.

Earl Grey strode around the table, showing off his new hat. The Mad Hatter clapped his hands, then asked, "Why is a mouse like a writing desk?"

"I don't know," Raven said. "Why is a mouse like a writing desk?"

The Mad Hatter scowled at her. "Whatever are you talking about? A mouse isn't one bit like a writing desk." He adjusted his polka-dot cravat. "Tea, anyone?"

"Yes, please!" Maddie said. All the chair cushions began to wiggle, as if trying to catch the girls' attention. Maddie and Raven chose the closest chairs and sat. Earl Grey scampered down the shelves and joined them.

"Flavor?" the Mad Hatter asked.

"Charmomile for me, and Earl Grey for Earl Grey," Maddie said.

"Dragonberry, please," Raven said.

The Mad Hatter tossed three saucers, teacups, and plates at the table. Each landed perfectly. Then three teapots flew from the kitchen and filled the guests' cups. A platter of frosted scones arrived, along with a pat of butter and a somewhat sleepy butter knife.

"Yum," Raven said, breaking a scone in half and dipping it into her tea. Earl Grey perched on his

saucer and carefully lapped at his tea, which was neither too hot nor too cold.

Maddie plopped two sugar cubes into the dormouse's cup, then frowned. "I'm sorry to say this, but without a vest and boots, you look quite normal."

Earl Grey's eyes widened. He darted beneath a checkered napkin.

"Poor little thing," Maddie said. "This won't do at all. I can't have my dearest friend in the whole world looking...*normal!*"

She would do anything to help her pet. They'd been together since they'd both arrived from Wonderland. At first, Maddie had felt alone at Ever After High. It had taken a while to make friends, but her dormouse had always been by her side. They liked the same things; they hummed the same songs. They were like two peas in a pod, or, as they say in Wonderland, two mad queens in a rose garden.

Raven pulled her MirrorPad from her book bag. "Let's see..." she said as she searched. "Mouse clothes. Where can we buy mouse clothes? Hmmm, nothing's popping up."

"You can't sit around and wait for a pot of tea to make itself," the Mad Hatter said.

Maddie beamed. "You're right! If we need a mouse vest, we should make it." Earl Grey poked his head out from under the napkin. He squeaked in agreement. "And then my mousey will be the opposite of ordinary. He'll be dapper again!"

"He'll be wonderlandiful," the Mad Hatter said. He pulled his overcoat from an oven, and a long scarf from a cookie jar. "Well, I'm off to a meeting of less importance than those of more importance, and so, toodle-doo." He opened the door. "And always remember, a tea leaves but a hat never does." Both Maddie and her father laughed. Then the Mad Hatter strolled down the cobbled lane.

Raven took a sip of her tea. "I don't mean to sound rude, but I only understand about half the things your dad says."

"Then you must work harder to understand less," Maddie told her with a shake of her finger. "Now, let's make some mousey clothes!"

"Uh, I'm not so good at sewing," Raven confessed.

"Me neither," Maddie said. "But not being good at something is no reason to worry. And Wonderland mice are natural tailors. They love to sew."

Because there were no other customers in the store, Maddie didn't fret about leaving it unsupervised. Besides, if someone walked in, the teapots would handle it. "Let's go to my dad's workshop," she said. With Earl Grey perched on her shoulder, she led Raven into the back room, where the Mad Hatter created his wondrous hats. Squares of felt, spools of ribbon, and feathers were scattered across the counters, along with buttons, bows, and beads. "What do we need?" she asked Earl Grey. He picked out a nice piece of plaid felt, a spool of thread, a needle, three brass buttons, and a pair of scissors.

Raven sat on a stool at the counter. "Aren't those buttons too big?" she asked.

"Everything's too big," Maddie realized as Earl Grey tried to pick up the scissors. "But I know what to do!"

Maddie set her hat on the table. It was called her Hat of Many Things because it had a magical secret. Maddie reached her hand into the hat, deeper and deeper, until her entire arm disappeared. "It's in here somewhere," she said, searching. Raven had seen this before. Maddie kept all sorts of stuff in that hat. But no matter how much she crammed into it, it never grew larger or heavier. "Oh, here it is." She pulled out a little vial with a label:

DRINK ME

"Is that what I think it is?" Raven asked worriedly.

"It's shrinking potion, from Wonderland. I always carry some, just in case. You never know when you might need to be two inches tall." She held it up to Raven's face.

"Wait a spell." Raven shook her head. "Have you flipped your crown? I'm not drinking that."

"Why would you drink it?" Maddie asked. She poured a drop of potion onto the scissors, the buttons, the needle and thread. In the blink of an eye, each of those items shrank down to perfect mouse size. "Ta-da!"

While Earl Grey set to work making himself a new vest, Maddie and Raven watched. He was a quick little fellow. In the time it took Raven to go back into the shop, grab another scone, return, and eat that scone, Earl Grey had cut the fabric and stitched the seams, all while humming a sweet tune.

A few customers came in. Maddie ran into the parlor, served tea and crumpets, then ran back. "He's made all the button holes," Raven reported. "Now he's attaching the buttons." Once he'd finished, he slipped into his vest, then walked down the counter as if it were a fashion show runway.

"Aw, he's so cute," Raven said.

"But he still looks a tiny bit normal," Maddie said. "We need one more thing."

The Glass Slipper Shoe Store was just down the street. Ashlynn Ella, quite the expert on shoes, found Maddie a new pair that was the exact same sparkly bluish green as Maddie's eyes. Earl Grey walked around the men's section. He looked at loafers, riding boots, and hiking boots, but then he crawled into a pair of soft leather boots and began squeaking.

"I think he likes these," Ashlynn said. "But I'm not sure we can order them in mouse size."

"No problem!" Maddie told her. She reached into her hat and pulled out the shrinking potion. One drop later, the boots were snug on Earl Grey's feet.

"Oh, Sir Mousey, you're a dapper dormouse indeed," Maddie said happily. "Why, you don't look one bit normal anymore. You look *abnormal*."

Raven laughed. "Are you sure that's the word you meant to say?"

"But I always mean what I say." Maddie giggled. "Or say what I mean. I get those confused."

Earl Grey didn't seem to care what word was used to describe his new look. He stepped outside, stood on the Glass Slipper's stoop with his paws on his hips, and puffed out his chest. He clearly liked his new outfit and wanted the world to see it.

"Oh, look at that cute dormouse," a lady said as she walked past.

"What a nice-looking gentleman," a man said.

"Eek, a mouse!" someone cried.

But it wasn't just the tall folk who noticed the nicely dressed mouse. Those who lived among the crevices and cracks, the hollows and holes, also took note.

And so it was that a few days later, when Maddie, Earl Grey, and Raven walked back to the Village of Book End to get a cup of tea, they were greeted with a funny little sight.

"I can't keep them in stock," the Mad Hatter exclaimed. A line of mice stood outside the Haberdashery and Tea Shoppe.

"Since when do village mice drink tea?" Raven asked.

"Not tea, not tea," the Mad Hatter said. "They all want hats!" He plucked three tiny hats from his pocket and tossed them out the door. Each hat landed on a mouse's head. Those three mice squeaked happily, then scampered away. Then the others in line began stomping their feet. "I'm making them as fast as I can!" the Mad Hatter cried as he rushed back to his workshop.

"Looks like you've started a trend," Raven told Earl Grey. "Now all the mice will look dapper." He removed his top hat and bowed.

"Well, that's hat-tastic!" Maddie said.

Acknowledgments

Writing all these stories about the Ever After High pets has brought to mind my own pets, past and present. As many of my readers know, I'm pretty crazy about dogs, but I admit there've been a few cats who've warmed my heart along the way. To the pets past, Lulu, Bonnie, Max, Buba, Mufasa, and Bean, and to the pets present, Skylos and Daisy, thanks for sharing the journey with me. Life would be rather boring without furballs and dog drool.

About the Author

$\mathcal{S}$uzanne Selfors feels like a Royal on some days and a Rebel on others. She's written many books for kids, including the Smells Like Dog series and the Imaginary Veterinary series.

She has two charming children and lives in a magical island kingdom, where she hopes it is her destiny to write stories forever after.

$\mathcal{C}$an't get enough Ever After High?
Keep reading about your
best friends forever after in
The School Story collection
by Suzanne Selfors: